A Rogue's Life

A Rogue's Life

Wilkie Collins

ET REMOTISSIMA PROPE

Hesperus Classics

Hesperus Classics
Published by Hesperus Press Limited
4 Rickett Street, London SW6 1RU
www.hesperuspress.com

First published in *Household Words* in 1856
First published by Hesperus Press Limited, 2006

Foreword © Peter Ackroyd, 2006

Designed and typeset by Fraser Muggeridge studio
Printed in Jordan by Jordan National Press

ISBN: 1-84391-132-9

CONTENTS

FOREWORD

Even at school Wilkie Collins assumed the part of the 'bad boy', and told a friend in later life that he was perpetually 'getting punished'; he was always held up to general obloquy as the model of undisciplined behaviour. This was the very best of starts for the author of *A Rogue's Life*. At school he also began a lifetime of storytelling, and used to entertain his young audience with tales of adventure and intrigue that were no doubt composed upon the spot. It was an aptitude that he would retain in his stories for the London periodicals, which have an unmistakeable air of having been invented *currente calamo*.

He began writing when he was apprenticed to a tea merchant in the Strand, and his first article was printed in the *Illuminated Magazine* of 1843. Collins was then just nineteen years old. This was the beginning of a career that was devoted almost entirely to literary pursuits. By the time he began to write *A Rogue's Life*, in 1855, he had composed two novels, several short stories and many general essays. He was also contributing to Charles Dickens' weekly periodical, *Household Words*, in which journal the separate episodes of *A Rogue's Life* first appeared in the early months of 1856. He had become a 'draw' to the general public, who appreciated his particular mixture of humour and adventure.

In these early years, in fact, he became a close associate and confidant of Charles Dickens. They had first met in the course of some amateur theatricals; it was a highly appropriate setting, since both of them possessed imaginations that were ringed by stage fire. They shared a common interest in the uncommon, and had an especial fondness for the oddities of urban existence. In the company of the older novelist – Dickens was some twelve years his senior – Collins made several journeys to Paris. They travelled there to enjoy what Dickens called the city's 'diableries' or, in the colloquial language of the period, to 'slum it'. They relaxed, went on various nocturnal excursions, and visited the more louche regions of the capital. They felt free. It was here, while residing at a Parisian hotel, that *A Rogue's Life* was written. In a preface to the published version of the novella, issued in 1879, Collins suggested that the 'almost boisterous gaiety' of the story had its origins in Paris. The sojourns there represented 'a very happy time in my life'. But the gaiety of *A Rogue's Life* may also be happily explained as the fluent expression of his native genius.

It is written in the first person, as a fictional autobiography. This is of course a literary device of long standing, employed by such able practitioners as Defoe and Dickens himself as well as by the more inventive journalists of the popular nineteenth-century magazines. But from the pen of Collins it becomes a thing of beauty. He has written a jovial satire upon the early years of the nineteenth century – the period seems to be that of the 1820s or thereabouts, the actual years never being revealed – and has anatomised a society in which the Rogue is the perpetual outsider. In just such a case was Collins himself, as a man with two mistresses and three illegitimate children. He and Dickens shared a genuine antipathy to the constraints of English civilisation, at least in its more 'polite' varieties, and the joy in this narrative comes from the Rogue's defiance of them. Collins had no regard for the more conventional proprieties, and paid no attention to what he calls in this novella 'the short-sighted eye of the world'.

The story is very much part of its period. The early nineteenth century was the age of the caricature and the character. It was an age of excessive stridency, theatricality and individualism – in all of which *A Rogue's Life* partakes. It is filled with striking portraits, from marchioness to maid, and is animated by an irresistible optimism and energy. It is highly appropriate therefore that the Rogue himself, Frank Softly, first finds employment as a caricaturist in the public prints. When he is consigned to debtors' jail, in the second chapter, he enters one of the enchanted worlds of nineteenth-century fiction. When there are also matters of wills and inheritance to consider, it is clear that Collins has fully reflected what used to be called the spirit of the age.

The novella is written with great facility and ingenuity, and the words give the impression of having almost literally flown from the pen of the author. Collins thoroughly enjoys his assumption of such a loose and amiable persona; he could in fact be said to be creating alternative lives for himself in the act of writing, which is one definition of the novelist's craft. He gives the unmistakeable impression, too, of making up the story as he goes along. It has too much the flavour of picaresque to have been conceived in advance. Here the novelist is the simple entertainer. Collins was once also described as 'the novelist who created sensation', by which is meant his deployment of mystery in *The Woman in White* and *The Moonstone*. Those novels came later, but there is more than a touch of their mood and atmosphere in the depiction here of the mysterious Doctor Dulcifer. His villainy, and charm, are very well done.

The serial nature of the original tale is displayed obviously enough in the dramatic anticipations of next week's instalment at the end of several chapters. Yet the adventure is real and compelling. Collins had an enviable gift for narrative, a natural predisposition for scenes of flight and pursuit, and a firm command of incident and intrigue. The nature of his writing invites instant attention. It is fluent, unforced and conversational; his ear for dialogue is very keen, and he has great skill at unobtrusive characterisation. He gets close to melodrama, but always manages to avoid it at the last possible moment.

A Rogue's Life remained one of his favourite stories. Dickens said of Collins that he was the one contemporary 'who would come ahead of all the field – being the only one who combined invention and power, both humorous and pathetic…'. These qualities are also to be found here. Although it is not the most important of Collins's fictions, it is one of the most engaging and most enthralling.

– Peter Ackroyd, 2006

INTRODUCTORY WORDS

The following pages were written more than twenty years since, and were then published periodically in *Household Words*.[1]

In the original form of publication the Rogue was very favourably received. Year after year, I delayed the republication, proposing, at the suggestion of my old friend, Mr Charles Reade,[2] to enlarge the present sketch of the hero's adventures in Australia. But the opportunity of carrying out this project has proved to be one of the lost opportunities of my life. I republish the story with its original conclusion unaltered, but with such occasional additions and improvements as will, I hope, render it more worthy of attention at the present time.

The critical reader may possibly notice a tone of almost boisterous gaiety in certain parts of these imaginary Confessions. I can only plead, in defence, that the story offers the faithful reflection of a very happy time in my past life. It was written at Paris, when I had Charles Dickens for a near neighbour and a daily companion, and when my leisure hours were joyously passed with many other friends, all associated with literature and art, of whom the admirable comedian, Regnier,[3] is now the only survivor. The revising of these pages has been to me a melancholy task. I can only hope that they may cheer the sad moments of others. The Rogue may surely claim two merits, at least, in the eyes of the new generation – he is never serious for two moments together, and he 'doesn't take long to read'.

– *W. C., Gloucester Place, London, 6th March, 1879*

A Rogue's Life

I

I am going to try if I can't write something about myself. My life has been rather a strange one. It may not seem particularly useful or respectable, but it has been, in some respects, adventurous; and that may give it claims to be read, even in the most prejudiced circles. I am an example of some of the workings of the social system of this illustrious country on the individual native, during the early part of the present century; and, if I may say so without unbecoming vanity, I should like to quote myself for the edification of my countrymen.

Who am I.

I am remarkably well connected, I can tell you. I came into this world with the great advantage of having Lady Malkinshaw for a grandmother, her ladyship's daughter for a mother, and Francis James Softly, Esq., MD (commonly called Dr Softly), for a father. I put my father last, because he was not so well connected as my mother, and my grandmother first, because she was the most nobly born person of the three. I have been, am still, and may continue to be, a Rogue; but I hope I am not abandoned enough yet to forget the respect that is due to rank.

On this account, I trust, nobody will show such want of regard for my feelings as to expect me to say much about my mother's brother. That inhuman person committed an outrage on his family by making a fortune in the soap and candle trade. I apologise for mentioning him, even in an accidental way. The fact is, he left my sister, Annabella, a legacy of rather a peculiar kind, saddled with certain conditions that indirectly affected me: but this passage of family history need not be produced just yet. I apologise a second time for alluding to money matters before it was absolutely necessary. Let me get back to

3

a pleasing and reputable subject by saying a word or two more about my father.

I am rather afraid that Dr Softly was not a clever medical man, for in spite of his great connections, he did not get a very magnificent practice as a physician.

As a general practitioner, he might have bought a comfortable business, with a house and snug surgery-shop attached; but the son-in-law of Lady Malkinshaw was obliged to hold up his head, and set up his carriage, and live in a street near a fashionable square, and keep an expensive and clumsy footman to answer the door, instead of a cheap and tidy housemaid. How he managed to 'maintain his position' (that is the right phrase, I think), I never could tell. His wife did not bring him a farthing. When the honourable and gallant baronet, her father, died, he left the widowed Lady Malkinshaw with her worldly affairs in a curiously involved state. Her son (of whom I feel truly ashamed to be obliged to speak again so soon) made an effort to extricate his mother – involved himself in a series of pecuniary disasters, which commercial people call, I believe, transactions – struggled for a little while to get out of them in the character of an independent gentleman – failed – and then spiritlessly availed himself of the oleaginous refuge of the soap and candle trade. His mother always looked down upon him after this, but borrowed money of him also – in order to show, I suppose, that her maternal interest in her son was not quite extinct. My father tried to follow her example – in his wife's interests, of course; but the soap-boiler brutally buttoned up his pockets, and told my father to go into business for himself. Thus it happened that we were certainly a poor family, in spite of the fine appearance we made, the fashionable street we lived in, the neat brougham we kept, and the clumsy and expensive footman who answered our door.

What was to be done with me in the way of education?

If my father had consulted his means, I should have been sent to a cheap commercial academy; but he had to consult his relationship to Lady Malkinshaw, so I was sent to one of the most fashionable and famous of the great public schools. I will not mention it by name, because I don't think the masters would be proud of my connection with it. I ran away three times, and was flogged three times. I made four aristocratic connections, and had four pitched battles with them: three thrashed me, and one I thrashed. I learned to play at cricket, to hate rich people, to cure warts, to write Latin verses, to swim, to recite speeches, to cook kidneys on toast, to draw caricatures of the masters, to construe Greek plays, to black boots, and to receive kicks and serious advice resignedly. Who will say that the fashionable public school was of no use to me after that?

After I left school, I had the narrowest escape possible of intruding myself into another place of accommodation for distinguished people: in other words, I was very nearly being sent to college. Fortunately for me, my father lost a lawsuit just in the nick of time, and was obliged to scrape together every farthing of available money that he possessed to pay for the luxury of going to law. If he could have saved his seven shillings, he would certainly have sent me to scramble for a place in the pit of the great university theatre; but his purse was empty, and his son was not eligible therefore for admission, in a gentlemanly capacity, at the doors.

The next thing was to choose a profession.

Here the doctor was liberality itself, in leaving me to my own devices. I was of a roving, adventurous temperament, and I should have liked to go into the army. But where was the money to come from, to pay for my commission? As to enlisting in the ranks and working my way up, the social institutions of my country obliged the grandson of Lady Malkinshaw to begin military life as an officer and gentleman, or not to begin it at all. The army, therefore, was out of the question. The Church? Equally out of the question, since I could not pay for admission to the prepared place of accommodation for distinguished people, and could not accept a charitable free pass, in consequence of my high connections. The Bar? I should be five years getting to it, and should have to spend two hundred a year in going circuit before I had earned a farthing. Physic? This really seemed the only gentlemanly refuge left; and yet, with the knowledge of my father's experience before me, I was ungrateful enough to feel a secret dislike for it. It is a degrading confession to make, but I remember wishing I was not so highly connected, and absolutely thinking that the life of a commercial traveller would have suited me exactly, if I had not been a poor gentleman. Driving about from place to place, living jovially at inns, seeing fresh faces constantly, and getting money by all this enjoyment, instead of spending it – what a life for me, if I had been the son of a haberdasher and the grandson of a groom's widow!

While my father was uncertain what to do with me, a new profession was suggested by a friend, which I shall repent not having been allowed to adopt to the last day of my life. This friend was an eccentric old gentleman of large property, much respected in our family. One day, my father, in my presence, asked his advice about the best manner of starting me in life, with due credit to my connections and sufficient advantage to myself.

'Listen to my experience,' said our eccentric friend, 'and, if you are a wise man, you will make up your mind as soon as you have heard me. I have three sons. I brought my eldest son up to the Church; he is said to be getting on admirably, and he costs me three hundred a year. I brought my second son up to the Bar; he is said to be getting on admirably, and he costs me four hundred a year. I brought my third son up to Quadrilles – he has married an heiress, and he costs me nothing.'

Ah, me! if that worthy sage's advice had only been followed – if I had been brought up to Quadrilles! – if I had only been cast loose on the ballrooms of London, to qualify under Hymen, for a golden degree! Oh! you young ladies with money, I was five feet ten in my stockings; I was great at small talk and dancing; I had glossy whiskers, curling locks, and a rich voice! Ye girls with golden guineas, ye nymphs with crisp banknotes, mourn over the husband you have lost among you – over the Rogue who has broken the laws that, as the partner of a landed or fund-holding woman, he might have helped to make on the benches of the British Parliament! Oh! ye hearths and homes sung about in so many songs – written about in so many books – shouted about in so many speeches, with accompaniment of so much loud cheering: what a settler on the hearthrug; what a possessor of property; what a bringer-up of a family was snatched away from you, when the son of Dr Softly was lost to the profession of Quadrilles!

It ended in my resigning myself to the misfortune of being a doctor.

If I was a very good boy and took pains, and carefully mixed in the best society, I might hope in the course of years to succeed to my father's brougham, fashionably situated house, and clumsy and expensive footman. There was a prospect for a lad of spirit, with the blood of the early Malkinshaws (who were Rogues of great capacity and distinction in the feudal times) coursing adventurous through every vein! I look back on my career, and when I remember the patience with which

7

I accepted a medical destiny, I appear to myself in the light of a hero. Nay, I even went beyond the passive virtue of accepting my destiny – I actually studied, I made the acquaintance of the skeleton, I was on friendly terms with the muscular system, and the mysteries of physiology dropped in on me in the kindest manner whenever they had an evening to spare.

Even this was not the worst of it. I disliked the abstruse studies of my new profession, but I absolutely hated the diurnal slavery of qualifying myself, in a social point of view, for future success in it. My fond medical parent insisted on introducing me to his whole connection. I went round visiting in the neat brougham – with a stethoscope and medical review in the front pocket, with Dr Softly by my side, keeping his face well in view at the window – to canvass for patients, in the character of my father's hopeful successor. Never have I been so ill at ease in prison as I was in that carriage. I have felt more at home in the dock (such is the natural depravity and perversity of my disposition) than ever I felt in the drawing rooms of my father's distinguished patrons and respectable friends. Nor did my miseries end with the morning calls. I was commanded to attend all dinner parties, and to make myself agreeable at all balls.

The dinners were the worst trial. Sometimes, indeed, we contrived to get ourselves asked to the houses of high and mighty entertainers, where we ate the finest French dishes and drank the oldest vintages, and fortified ourselves sensibly and snugly in that way against the frigidity of the company. Of these repasts I have no hard words to say; it is of the dinners we gave ourselves, and of the dinners that people in our rank of life gave to us, that I now bitterly complain.

Have you ever observed the remarkable adherence to set forms of speech that characterises the talkers of arrant nonsense! Precisely the same sheepish following of one given example distinguishes the ordering of genteel dinners.

When we gave a dinner at home, we had gravy soup, turbot and lobster-sauce, haunch of mutton, boiled fowls and tongue, lukewarm oyster-patties and sticky curry for side dishes; wild duck, cabinet pudding, jelly, cream and tartlets. All excellent things, except when you have to eat them continually. We lived upon them entirely in the season. Every one of our hospitable friends gave us a return dinner, which was a perfect copy of ours – just as ours was a perfect copy of theirs, last year. They boiled what we boiled, and we roasted what they roasted. We none of us ever changed the succession of the courses – or made more or less of them – or altered the position of the fowls opposite the mistress and the haunch opposite the master. My stomach used to quail within me, in those times, when the tureen was taken off and the inevitable gravy-soup smell renewed its daily acquaintance with my nostrils, and warned me of the persistent eatable formalities that were certain to follow. I suppose that honest people, who have known what it is to get no dinner (being a Rogue, I have myself never wanted for one), have gone through some very acute suffering under that privation. It may be some consolation to them to know that, next to absolute starvation, the same company-dinner, every day, is one of the hardest trials that assail human endurance. I date my first serious determination to throw over the medical profession at the earliest convenient opportunity from the second season's series of dinners at which my aspirations, as a rising physician, unavoidably and regularly condemned me to be present.

II

The opportunity I wanted presented itself in a curious way, and led, unexpectedly enough, to some rather important consequences.

I have already stated, among the other branches of human attainment that I acquired at the public school, that I learned to draw caricatures of the masters who were so obliging as to educate me. I had a natural faculty for this useful department of art. I improved it greatly by practice in secret after I left school, and I ended by making it a source of profit and pocket money to me when I entered the medical profession. What was I to do? I could not expect for years to make a halfpenny as a physician. My genteel walk in life led me away from all immediate sources of emolument, and my father could only afford to give me an allowance that was too preposterously small to be mentioned. I had helped myself surreptitiously to pocket money at school, by selling my caricatures, and I was obliged to repeat the process at home!

At the time of which I write, the art of caricature was just approaching the close of its coloured and most extravagant stage of development. The subtlety and truth to nature required for the pursuit of it now had hardly begun to be thought of then. Sheer farce and coarse burlesque, with plenty of colour for the money, still made up the sum of what the public of those days wanted. I was first assured of my capacity for the production of these requisites by a medical friend of the ripe critical age of nineteen. He knew a print-publisher, and enthusiastically showed him a portfolio full of my sketches, taking care at my request not to mention my name. Rather to my surprise (for I was too conceited to be greatly amazed by the circumstance), the publisher picked out a few of the best of my wares, and boldly bought them of me – of course, at his own price. From that time I became, in an anonymous way, one of the young buccaneers of British caricature, cruising about here, there and everywhere, at all my intervals of spare time, for any prize in the shape of a subject that it was possible to pick up. Little did my highly connected mother think that, among the coloured prints in the shop-window, which disrespectfully illustrated the public and private proceedings of distinguished individuals, certain specimens bearing the classic signature of 'Thersites Junior' were produced from designs furnished by her studious and medical son. Little did my respectable father imagine when, with great difficulty and vexation, he succeeded in getting me now and then smuggled, along with himself, inside the pale of fashionable society – that he was helping me to study likenesses that were destined under my reckless treatment to make the public laugh at some of his most august patrons, and to fill the pockets of his son with professional fees, never once dreamed of in his philosophy.

For more than a year I managed, unsuspected, to keep the privy purse fairly supplied by the exercise of my caricaturing abilities. But the day of detection was to come.

Whether my medical friend's admiration of my satirical sketches led him into talking about them in public with too little reserve, or whether the servants at home found private means of watching me in my moments of art study, I know not: but that someone betrayed me, and that the discovery of my illicit manufacture of caricatures was actually communicated even to the grandmotherly head and fount of the family honour, is a most certain and lamentable matter of fact. One morning my father received a letter from Lady Malkinshaw herself, informing him, in a handwriting crooked with poignant grief, and blotted at every third word by the violence of virtuous indignation, that 'Thersites Junior' was his own son, and that, in one of the last of the 'ribald's' caricatures, her own venerable features were unmistakably represented as belonging to the body of a large owl!

Of course, I laid my hand on my heart and indignantly denied everything. Useless. My original model for the owl had got proofs of my guilt that were not to be resisted.

The doctor, ordinarily the most mellifluous and self-possessed of men, flew into a violent, roaring, cursing passion on this occasion – declared that I was imperilling the honour and standing of the family – insisted on my never drawing another caricature, either for public or private purposes, as long as I lived, and ordered me to go forthwith and ask pardon of Lady Malkinshaw in the humblest terms that it was possible to select. I answered dutifully that I was quite ready to obey, on the condition that he should reimburse me by a trebled allowance for what I should lose by giving up the art of caricature, or that Lady Malkinshaw should confer on me the appointment of physician-in-waiting on her, with a handsome salary attached. These extremely moderate stipulations so increased my father's anger that he asserted, with an unmentionably vulgar oath, his resolution to turn me out of doors if I did not do as he bid me, without daring to hint at any conditions whatsoever. I bowed, and said that I would save him the exertion of turning me out of doors, by going of my own accord. He shook his fist at me, after which it obviously became my duty, as a member of a gentlemanly and peaceful profession, to leave the room. The same evening I left the house, and I have never once given the clumsy and expensive footman the trouble of answering the door to me since that time.

I have reason to believe that my exodus from home was, on the whole, favourably viewed by my mother, as tending to remove any possibility of my bad character and conduct interfering with my sister's advancement in life.

By dint of angling with great dexterity and patience, under the direction of both her parents, my handsome sister Annabella had succeeded in catching an eligible husband, in the shape of a wizen, miserly, mahogany-coloured man, turned fifty, who had made a fortune in the West Indies. His name was Batterbury; he had been dried up under a tropical sun, so as to look as if he would keep for ages; he had two subjects of conversation, the yellow-fever and the advantage of walking exercise; and he was barbarian enough to take a violent dislike to me. He had proved a very delicate fish to hook, and, even when Annabella had caught him, my father and mother had great difficulty in landing him – principally, they were good enough to say, in consequence of my presence on the scene. Hence the decided advantage of my removal from home. It is a very pleasant reflection to me, now, to remember how disinterestedly I studied the good of my family in those early days.

Abandoned entirely to my own resources, I naturally returned to the business of caricaturing with renewed ardour.

About this time Thersites Junior really began to make something like a reputation, and to walk abroad habitually with a banknote comfortably lodged among the other papers in his pocketbook. For a year I lived a gay and glorious life in some of the freest society in London; at the end of that time, my tradesmen, without any provocation on my part, sent in their bills. I found myself in the very absurd position of having no money to pay them, and told them all so with the frankness that is one of the best sides of my character. They received my advances toward a better understanding with brutal incivility, and treated me soon afterward with a want of confidence that

I may forgive, but can never forget. One day, a dirty stranger touched me on the shoulder, and showed me a dirty slip of paper that I at first presumed to be his card. Before I could tell him what a vulgar document it looked like, two more dirty strangers put me into a hackney coach. Before I could prove to them that this proceeding was a gross infringement on the liberties of the British subject, I found myself lodged within the walls of a prison.

Well! and what of that? Who am I that I should object to being in prison, when so many of the royal personages and illustrious characters of history have been there before me? Can I not carry on my vocation in greater comfort here than I could in my father's house? Have I any anxieties outside these walls? No: for my beloved sister is married – the family net has landed Mr Batterbury at last. No: for I read in the paper the other day that Dr Softly (doubtless through the interest of Lady Malkinshaw) has been appointed the King's-Barber-Surgeon's-Deputy-Consulting Physician. My relatives are comfortable in their sphere – let me proceed forthwith to make myself comfortable in mine. Pen, ink, and paper, if you please, Mr Jailer: I wish to write to my esteemed publisher.

DEAR SIR – Please advertise a series of twelve racy prints, from my fertile pencil, entitled, 'Scenes of Modern Prison Life', by Thersites Junior. The two first designs will be ready by the end of the week, to be paid for on delivery, according to the terms settled between us for my previous publications of the same size.

With great regard and esteem, faithfully yours,

– FRANK SOFTLY

Having thus provided for my support in prison, I was enabled to introduce myself to my fellow-debtors, and to study character for the new series of prints, on the very first day of my incarceration, with my mind quite at ease.

If the reader desires to make acquaintance with the associates of my captivity, I must refer him to 'Scenes of Modern Prison Life', by Thersites Junior, now doubtless extremely scarce, but producible to the demands of patience and perseverance, I should imagine, if anybody will be so obliging as to pass a week or so over the catalogue of the British Museum. My fertile pencil has delineated the characters I met with, at that period of my life, with a force and distinctness that my pen cannot hope to rival – has portrayed them all more or less prominently, with the one solitary exception of a prisoner called Gentleman Jones. The reasons why I excluded him from my portrait gallery are so honourable to both of us that I must ask permission briefly to record them.

My fellow-captives soon discovered that I was studying their personal peculiarities for my own advantage and for the public amusement. Some thought the thing a good joke; some objected to it, and quarrelled with me. Liberality in the matter of liquor and small loans reconciled a large proportion of the objectors to their fate; the sulky minority I treated with contempt, and scourged avengingly with the smart lash of caricature. I was at that time probably the most impudent man of my age in all England, and the common flock of jail-birds quailed before the magnificence of my assurance. One prisoner only set me and my pencil successfully at defiance. That prisoner was Gentleman Jones.

He had received his name from the suavity of his countenance, the inveterate politeness of his language, and the unassailable composure of his manner. He was in the prime of life, but very bald – had been in the army and the coal trade – wore very stiff collars and prodigiously long wristbands – seldom laughed, but talked with remarkable glibness, and was never known to lose his temper under the most aggravating circumstances of prison existence.

He abstained from interfering with me and my studies, until it was reported in our society, that in the sixth print of my series, Gentleman Jones, highly caricatured, was to form one of the principal figures. He then appealed to me personally and publicly, on the racket-ground, in the following terms:

'Sir,' said he, with his usual politeness and his unwavering smile, 'you will greatly oblige me by not caricaturing my personal peculiarities. I am so unfortunate as not to possess a sense of humour, and if you did my likeness, I am afraid I should not see the joke of it.'

'Sir,' I returned, with my customary impudence, 'it is not of the slightest importance whether *you* see the joke of it or not. The public will – and that is enough for me.'

With that civil speech, I turned on my heel, and the prisoners near all burst out laughing. Gentleman Jones, not in the least altered or ruffled, smoothed down his wristbands, smiled, and walked away.

The same evening I was in my room alone, designing the new print, when there came a knock at the door, and Gentleman Jones walked in. I got up, and asked what the devil he wanted. He smiled, and turned up his long wristbands.

'Only to give you a lesson in politeness,' said Gentleman Jones.

'What do you mean, sir? How dare you – ?'

The answer was a smart slap on the face. I instantly struck out in a state of fury – was stopped with great neatness – and received in return a blow on the head, which sent me down on the carpet half stunned, and too giddy to know the difference between the floor and the ceiling.

'Sir,' said Gentleman Jones, smoothing down his wristbands again, and addressing me blandly as I lay on the floor, 'I have the honour to inform you that you have now received your first lesson in politeness. Always be civil to those who are civil to you. The little matter of the caricature we will settle on a future occasion. I wish you good evening.'

The noise of my fall had been heard by the other occupants of rooms on my landing. Most fortunately for my dignity, they did not come in to see what was the matter until I had been able to get into my chair again. When they entered, I felt that the impression of the slap was red on my face still, but the mark of the blow was hidden by my hair. Under these fortunate circumstances, I was able to keep up my character among my friends, when they enquired about the scuffle, by informing them that Gentleman Jones had audaciously slapped my face, and that I had been obliged to retaliate by knocking him down. My word in the prison was as good as his, and if my version of the story got fairly the start of his, I had the better chance of the two of being believed.

I was rather anxious, the next day, to know what course my polite and pugilistic instructor would take. To my utter amazement, he bowed to me as civilly as usual when we met in the yard; he never denied my version of the story; and when my friends laughed at him as a thrashed man, he took not the slightest notice of their agreeable merriment. Antiquity, I think, furnishes us with few more remarkable characters than Gentleman Jones.

That evening I thought it desirable to invite a friend to pass the time with me. As long as my liquor lasted he stopped;

when it was gone, he went away. I was just locking the door after him, when it was pushed open gently, but very firmly, and Gentleman Jones walked in.

My pride, which had not allowed me to apply for protection to the prison authorities, would not allow me now to call for help. I tried to get to the fireplace and arm myself with the poker, but Gentleman Jones was too quick for me. 'I have come, sir, to give you a lesson in morality tonight,' he said, and up went his right hand.

I stopped the preliminary slap, but before I could hit him, his terrible left fist reached my head again, and down I fell once more – upon the hearthrug this time – not over-heavily.

'Sir,' said Gentleman Jones, making me a bow, 'you have now received your first lesson in morality. Always speak the truth, and never say what is false of another man behind his back. Tomorrow, with your kind permission, we will finally settle the adjourned question of the caricature. Goodnight.'

I was far too sensible a man to leave the settling of that question to him. The first thing in the morning I sent a polite note to Gentleman Jones, informing him that I had abandoned all idea of exhibiting his likeness to the public in my series of prints, and giving him full permission to inspect every design I made before it went out of the prison. I received a most civil answer, thanking me for my courtesy, and complimenting me on the extraordinary aptitude with which I profited by the most incomplete and elementary instruction. I thought I deserved the compliment, and I think so still. Our conduct, as I have already intimated, was honourable to us, on either side. It was honourable attention on the part of Gentleman Jones to correct me when I was in error; it was honourable common sense in me to profit by the correction. I have never seen this great man since he compounded with his creditors and got out of prison, but my feelings toward him are still those of profound gratitude and respect. He gave me the only useful teaching I ever had; and if this should meet the eye of Gentleman Jones I hereby thank him for beginning and ending my education in two evenings, without costing me or my family a single farthing.

III

To return to my business affairs. When I was comfortably settled in the prison, and knew exactly what I owed, I thought it my duty to my father to give him the first chance of getting me out. His answer to my letter contained a quotation from Shakespeare on the subject of thankless children, but no remittance of money. After that, my only course was to employ a lawyer and be declared a bankrupt. I was most uncivilly treated, and remanded two or three times. When everything I possessed had been sold for the benefit of my creditors, I was reprimanded and let out. It is pleasant to think that, even then, my faith in myself and in human nature was still not shaken.

About ten days before my liberation, I was thunderstruck at receiving a visit from my sister's mahogany-coloured husband, Mr Batterbury. When I was respectably settled at home, this gentleman would not so much as look at me without a frown, and now, when I was a scamp, in prison, he mercifully and fraternally came to condole with me on my misfortunes. A little dexterous questioning disclosed the secret of this prodigious change in our relations toward each other, and informed me of a family event that altered my position toward my sister in the most whimsical manner.

While I was being removed to the bankruptcy court, my uncle in the soap and candle trade was being removed to the other world. His will took no notice of my father or my mother, but he left to my sister (always supposed to be his favourite in the family) a most extraordinary legacy of possible pin money, in the shape of a contingent reversion to the sum of three thousand pounds, payable on the death of Lady Malkinshaw, provided I survived her.

Whether this document sprang into existence out of any of his involved money transactions with his mother was more than Mr Batterbury could tell. I could ascertain nothing in relation to it, except that the bequest was accompanied by some cynical remarks, to the effect that the testator would feel happy if his legacy were instrumental in reviving the dormant interest of only one member of Dr Softly's family in the fortunes of the hopeful young gentleman who had run away from home. My esteemed uncle evidently felt that he could not in common decency avoid doing something for his sister's family, and he had done it accordingly in the most malicious and mischievous manner. This was characteristic of him: he was just the man, if he had not possessed the document before, to have had it drawn out on his deathbed for the amiable purpose that it was now devoted to serve.

Here was a pretty complication! Here was my sister's handsome legacy made dependent on my outliving my grandmother! This was diverting enough, but Mr Batterbury's conduct was more amusing still.

The miserly little wretch not only tried to conceal his greedy desire to save his own pockets by securing the allowance of pin money left to his wife, but absolutely persisted in ignoring the plain fact that his visit to me sprang from the serious pecuniary interest that he and Annabella now had in the life and health of your humble servant. I made all the necessary jokes about the strength of the vital principle in Lady Malkinshaw, and the broken condition of my own constitution, but he solemnly abstained from understanding one of them. He resolutely kept up appearances in the very face of detection; not the faintest shade of red came over his wicked old mahogany face as he told me how shocked he and his wife were at my present position, and how anxious

Annabella was that he should not forget to give me her love. Tender-hearted creature! I had only been in prison six months when that overwhelming testimony of sisterly affection came to console me in my captivity. Ministering angel! you shall get your three thousand pounds. I am fifty years younger than Lady Malkinshaw, and I will take care of myself, Annabella, for thy dear sake!

The next time I saw Mr Batterbury was on the day when I at last got my discharge. He was not waiting to see where I was going next, or what vital risks I was likely to run on the recovery of my freedom, but to congratulate me, and to give me Annabella's love. It was a very gratifying attention, and I said as much, in tones of the deepest feeling.

'How is dear Lady Malkinshaw?' I asked, when my grateful emotions had subsided.

Mr Batterbury shook his head mournfully. 'I regret to say, not quite so well as her friends could wish,' he answered. 'The last time I had the pleasure of seeing her ladyship, she looked so yellow that if we had been in Jamaica I should have said it was a case of death in twelve hours. I respectfully endeavoured to impress upon her ladyship the necessity of keeping the functions of the liver active by daily walking exercise: time, distance, and pace being regulated with proper regard to her age – you understand me? – of course, with proper regard to her age.'

'You could not possibly have given her better advice,' I said. 'When I saw her, as long as two years ago, Lady Malkinshaw's favourite delusion was that she was the most active woman of seventy-five in all England. She used to tumble downstairs two or three times a week, then, because she never would allow any one to help her, and could not be brought to believe that she was as blind as a mole, and as rickety on her legs as a child of a year old. Now you have encouraged her to take to walking, she will be more obstinate than ever, and is sure to tumble down daily, out of doors as well as in. Not even the celebrated Malkinshaw toughness can last out more than a few weeks of that practice. Considering the present shattered condition of my constitution, you couldn't have given her better advice – upon my word of honour, you couldn't have given her better advice!'

'I am afraid,' said Mr Batterbury, with a power of face I envied, 'I am afraid, my dear Frank (let me call you Frank), that I don't quite apprehend your meaning; and we have unfortunately no time to enter into explanations. Five miles here by a roundabout way is only half my daily allowance of walking exercise; five miles back by a roundabout way remain to be now accomplished. So glad to see you at liberty again! Mind you let us know where you settle, and take care of yourself, and do recognise the importance to the whole animal economy of daily walking exercise – do now! Did I give you Annabella's love? She's so well. Goodbye.'

Away went Mr Batterbury to finish his walk for the sake of his health, and away went I to visit my publisher for the sake of my pocket.

An unexpected disappointment awaited me. My 'Scenes of Modern Prison Life' had not sold so well as had been anticipated, and my publisher was gruffly disinclined to speculate in any future works done in the same style. During the time of my imprisonment, a new caricaturist had started, with a manner of his own; he had already formed a new school, and the fickle public were all running together after him and his disciples. I said to myself: 'This scene in the drama of your life, my friend, has closed in; you must enter on another, or drop the curtain at once.' Of course I entered on another.

Taking leave of my publisher, I went to consult an artist-friend on my future prospects. I supposed myself to be merely on my way to a change of profession. As destiny ordered it, I was also on my way to the woman who was not only to be the object of my first love, but the innocent cause of the great disaster of my life.

I first saw her in one of the narrow streets leading from Leicester Square to the Strand. There was something in her face (dimly visible behind a thick veil) that instantly stopped me as I passed her. I looked back and hesitated. Her figure was the perfection of modest grace. I yielded to the impulse of the moment. In plain words, I did what you would have done, in my place – I followed her.

She looked round – discovered me – and instantly quickened her pace. Reaching the westward end of the Strand, she crossed the street and suddenly entered a shop.

I looked through the window, and saw her speak to a respectable elderly person behind the counter, who darted an indignant look at me, and at once led my charming stranger into a back office. For the moment, I was fool enough to feel puzzled; it was out of my character you will say – but remember, all men are fools when they first fall in love. After a little while I recovered the use of my senses. The shop was at the corner of a side street, leading to the market, since removed to make room for the railway. 'There's a back entrance to the house!' I thought to myself – and ran down the side street. Too late! the lovely fugitive had escaped me. Had I lost her forever in the great world of London? I thought so at the time. Events will show that I never was more mistaken in my life.

I was in no humour to call on my friend. It was not until another day had passed that I sufficiently recovered my composure to see poverty staring me in the face, and to understand that I had really no alternative but to ask the good-natured artist to lend me a helping hand.

I had heard it darkly whispered that he was something of a vagabond. But the term is so loosely applied, and it seems so difficult, after all, to define what a vagabond is, or to strike the right moral balance between the vagabond work that is boldly published and the vagabond work that is reserved for private circulation only, that I did not feel justified in holding aloof from my former friend. Accordingly, I renewed our acquaintance, and told him my present difficulty. He was a sharp man, and he showed me a way out of it directly.

'You have a good eye for a likeness,' he said, 'and you have made it keep you hitherto. Very well. Make it keep you still. You can't profitably caricature people's faces any longer – never mind! go to the other extreme, and flatter them now. Turn portrait-painter. You shall have the use of this study three days in the week, for ten shillings a week – sleeping on the hearthrug included, if you like. Get your paints, rouse up your friends, set to work at once. Drawing is of no consequence; painting is of no consequence; perspective is of no consequence; ideas are of no consequence. Everything is of no consequence, except catching a likeness and flattering your sitter – and that you know you can do.'

I felt that I could, and left him for the nearest colourman's.

Before I got to the shop, I met Mr Batterbury taking his walking exercise. He stopped, shook hands with me affectionately, and asked where I was going. A wonderful idea struck me. Instead of answering his question, I asked after Lady Malkinshaw.

'Don't be alarmed,' said Mr Batterbury; 'her ladyship tumbled downstairs yesterday morning.'

'My dear sir, allow me to congratulate you!'

'Most fortunately,' continued Mr Batterbury, with a strong emphasis on the words and a fixed stare at me, 'most fortunately, the servant had been careless enough to leave a large bundle of clothes for the wash at the foot of the stairs, while she went to answer the door. Falling headlong from the landing, her ladyship pitched (pardon me the expression) – pitched into the very middle of the bundle. She was a little shaken at the time, but is reported to be going on charmingly this morning. Most fortunate, was it not? Seen the papers? Awful news from Demerara – the yellow fever – '

'I wish I was at Demerara,' I said, in a hollow voice.

'You! Why?' exclaimed Mr Batterbury, aghast.

'I am homeless, friendless, penniless,' I went on, getting more hollow at every word. 'All my intellectual instincts tell me that I could retrieve my position and live respectably in the world, if I might only try my hand at portrait-painting – the thing of all others that I am naturally fittest for. But I have nobody to start me; no sitter to give me a first chance; nothing in my pocket but three-and-sixpence; and nothing in my mind but a doubt whether I shall struggle on a little longer, or end it immediately in the Thames. Don't let me detain you from your walk, my dear sir. I'm afraid Lady Malkinshaw will outlive me, after all!'

'Stop!' cried Mr Batterbury, his mahogany face actually getting white with alarm. 'Stop! Don't talk in that dreadfully unprincipled manner – don't, I implore, I insist! You have plenty of friends – you have me, and your sister. Take to portrait-painting – think of your family, and take to portrait-painting!'

'Where am I to get a sitter?' I enquired, with a gloomy shake of the head.

'Me,' said Mr Batterbury, with an effort. 'I'll be your first sitter. As a beginner, and especially to a member of the family, I suppose your terms will be moderate. Small beginnings – you know the proverb?' Here he stopped, and a miserly leer puckered up his mahogany cheeks.

'I'll do you, life-size, down to your waistcoat, for fifty pounds,' said I.

Mr Batterbury winced, and looked about him to the right and left, as if he wanted to run away. He had five thousand a year, but he contrived to look, at that moment, as if his utmost income was five hundred. I walked on a few steps.

'Surely those terms are rather high to begin with?' he said, walking after me. 'I should have thought five-and-thirty, or perhaps forty – '

'A gentleman, sir, cannot condescend to bargain,' said I, with mournful dignity. 'Farewell!' I waved my hand, and crossed over the way.

'Don't do that!' cried Mr Batterbury. 'I accept. Give me your address. I'll come tomorrow. Will it include the frame? There! there! it doesn't include the frame, of course. Where are you going now? To the colourman? He doesn't live in the Strand, I hope – or near one of the bridges. Think of Annabella, think of the family, think of the fifty pounds – an income, a year's income to a prudent man. Pray, pray be careful, and compose your mind; promise me, my dear, dear fellow – promise me, on your word of honour, to compose your mind!'

I left him still harping on that string, and suffering, I believe, the only serious attack of mental distress that had ever affected him in the whole course of his life.

Behold me, then, now starting afresh in the world, in the character of a portrait-painter, with the payment of my remuneration from my first sitter depending whimsically on the life of my grandmother. If you care to know how Lady Malkinshaw's health got on, and how I succeeded in my new profession, you have only to follow the further course of these confessions, in the next chapter.

IV

I gave my orders to the colourman, and settled matters with my friend the artist that day.

The next morning, before the hour at which I expected my sitter, having just now as much interest in the life of Lady Malkinshaw as Mr Batterbury had in her death, I went to make kind enquiries after her ladyship's health. The answer was most reassuring. Lady Malkinshaw had no present intention of permitting me to survive her. She was, at that very moment, meritoriously and heartily engaged in eating her breakfast. My prospects being now of the best possible kind, l felt encouraged to write once more to my father, telling him of my fresh start in life, and proposing a renewal of our acquaintance. I regret to say that he was so rude as not to answer my letter.

Mr Batterbury was punctual to the moment. He gave a gasp of relief when he beheld me, full of life, with my palette on my thumb, gazing fondly on my new canvas.

'That's right!' he said. 'I like to see you with your mind composed. Annabella would have come with me, but she has a little headache this morning. She sends her love and best wishes.'

I seized my chalks and began with that confidence in myself that has never forsaken me in any emergency. Being perfectly well aware of the absolute dependence of the art of portrait-painting on the art of flattery, I determined to start with making the mere outline of my likeness a compliment to my sitter.

It was much easier to resolve on doing this than really to do it. In the first place, my hand would relapse into its wicked old caricaturing habits. In the second place, my brother-in-law's face was so inveterately and completely ugly as to set every artifice of pictorial improvement at flat defiance. When a man has a nose an inch long, with the nostrils set perpendicularly, it is impossible to flatter it – you must either change it into a fancy nose, or resignedly acquiesce in it. When a man has no perceptible eyelids, and when his eyes globularly project so far out of his head that you expect to have to pick them up for him whenever you see him lean forward, how are mortal fingers and brushes to diffuse the right complimentary expression over them? You must either do them the most hideous and complete justice, or give them up altogether. The late Sir Thomas Lawrence, PRA, was undoubtedly the most artful and uncompromising flatterer that ever smoothed out all the natural characteristic blemishes from a sitter's face, but even that accomplished parasite would have found Mr Batterbury too much for him, and would have been driven, for the first time in his practice of art, to the uncustomary and uncourtly resource of absolutely painting a genuine likeness.

As for me, I put my trust in Lady Malkinshaw's power of living, and portrayed the face of Mr Batterbury in all its native horror. At the same time, I sensibly guarded against even the most improbable accidents by making him pay me the fifty pounds as we went on, by instalments. We had ten sittings. Each one of them began with a message from Mr Batterbury, giving me Annabella's love and apologies for not being able to come and see me. Each one of them ended with an argument between Mr Batterbury and me relative to the transfer of five pounds from his pocket to mine. I came off victorious on every occasion – being backed by the noble behaviour of Lady Malkinshaw, who abstained from tumbling down, and who ate and drank, and slept and grew lusty, for three weeks together. Venerable woman! She put fifty pounds into my pocket. I shall think of her with gratitude and respect to the end of my days.

One morning, while I was sitting before my completed portrait, inwardly shuddering over the ugliness of it, a suffocating smell of musk was wafted into the studio. It was followed by a sound of rustling garments, and that again was succeeded by the personal appearance of my affectionate sister, with her husband at her heels. Annabella had got to the end of her stock of apologies, and had come to see me.

She put her handkerchief to her nose the moment she entered the room.

'How do you do, Frank? Don't kiss me: you smell of paint, and I can't bear it.'

I felt a similar antipathy to the smell of musk, and had not the slightest intention of kissing her, but I was too gallant a man to say so, and I only begged her to favour me by looking at her husband's portrait.

Annabella glanced all round the room, with her handkerchief still at her nose, and gathered her magnificent silk dress close about her superb figure with her disengaged hand.

'What a horrid place!' she said faintly behind her handkerchief. 'Can't you take some of the paint away? I'm sure there's oil on the floor. How am I to get past that nasty table with the palette on it? Why can't you bring the picture down to the carriage, Frank?'

Advancing a few steps, and looking suspiciously about her while she spoke, her eyes fell on the chimney-piece. An eau de Cologne bottle stood upon it, which she took up immediately with a languishing sigh.

It contained turpentine for washing brushes in. Before I could warn her, she had sprinkled herself absently with half the contents of the bottle. In spite of all the musk that now filled the room, the turpentine betrayed itself almost as soon as I cried 'Stop!' Annabella, with a shriek of disgust, flung the bottle furiously into the fireplace. Fortunately it was summertime, or I might have had to echo the shriek with a cry of 'Fire!'

'You wretch! you brute! you low, mischievous, swindling blackguard!' cried my amiable sister, shaking her skirts with all her might, 'you have done this on purpose! Don't tell me! I know you have. What do you mean by pestering me to come to this dog-kennel of a place?' she continued, turning fiercely upon the partner of her existence and legitimate receptacle of all her superfluous wrath. 'What do you mean by bringing me here to see how you have been swindled? Yes, sir, swindled! He has no more idea of painting than you have. He has cheated you out of your money. If he was starving tomorrow he would be the last man in England to make away with himself – he is too great a wretch – he is too vicious – he is too lost to all sense of respectability – he is too much of a discredit to his family. Take me away! Give me your arm directly! I told you not to go near him from the first. This is what comes of your horrid fondness for money. Suppose Lady Malkinshaw does outlive him; suppose I do lose my legacy. What is three thousand pounds to you? My dress is ruined. My shawl's spoiled. *He* die! If the old woman lives to the age of Methuselah, he won't die. Give me your arm. No! Go to my father. I want medical advice. My nerves are torn to pieces. I'm giddy, faint, sick – SICK, Mr Batterbury!'

Here she became hysterical, and vanished, leaving a mixed odour of musk and turpentine behind her, which preserved the memory of her visit for nearly a week afterward.

'Another scene in the drama of my life seems likely to close in before long,' thought I. 'No chance now of getting my amiable sister to patronise struggling genius. Do I know of anybody else who will sit to me? No, not a soul. Having thus no portraits of other people to paint, what is it my duty, as a neglected artist, to do next? Clearly to take a portrait of myself.'

I did so, making my own likeness quite a pleasant relief to the ugliness of my brother-in-law's. It was my intention to send both portraits to the Royal Academy Exhibition, to get custom and show the public generally what I could do. I knew the institution with which I had to deal, and called my own likeness *Portrait of a Nobleman*.

That dexterous appeal to the tenderest feelings of my distinguished countrymen very nearly succeeded. The portrait of Mr Batterbury (much the more carefully painted picture of the two) was summarily turned out. The Portrait of a Nobleman was politely reserved to be hung up, if the Royal Academicians could possibly find room for it. They could not. So that picture also vanished back into the obscurity of the artist's easel. Weak and well-meaning people would have desponded under these circumstances, but your genuine Rogue is a man of elastic temperament, not easily compressible under any pressure of disaster. I sent the portrait of Mr Batterbury to the house of that distinguished patron, and the *Portrait of a Nobleman* to the pawnbroker's. After this I had plenty of elbow room in the studio, and could walk up and down briskly, smoking my pipe, and thinking about what I should do next.

I had observed that the generous friend and vagabond brother artist, whose lodger I now was, never seemed to be in absolute want of money; and yet the walls of his studio informed me that nobody bought his pictures. There hung all his great works, rejected by the Royal Academy, and neglected by the patrons of art; and there, nevertheless, was he, blithely plying the brush; not rich, it is true, but certainly never without money enough in his pocket for the supply of all his modest wants. Where did he find his resources? I determined to ask him the question the very next time he came to the studio.

'Dick,' I said (we called each other by our Christian names), 'where do you get your money?'

'Frank,' he answered, 'what makes you ask that question?'

'Necessity,' I proceeded. 'My stock of money is decreasing, and I don't know how to replenish it. My pictures have been turned out of the exhibition-rooms; nobody comes to sit to me; I can't make a farthing; and I must try another line in the arts, or leave your studio. We are old friends now. I've paid you honestly week by week, and if you can oblige me, I think you ought. You earn money somehow. Why can't I?'

'Are you at all particular?' asked Dick.

'Not in the least,' I answered.

Dick nodded, and looked pleased, handed me my hat, and put on his own.

'You are just the sort of man I like,' he remarked, 'and I would sooner trust you than anyone else I know. You ask how I contrive to earn money, seeing that all my pictures are still in my own possession. My dear fellow, whenever my pockets are empty, and I want a ten-pound note to put into them, I make an old master.'

I stared hard at him, not at first quite understanding what he meant.

'The old master I can make best,' continued Dick, 'is Claude Lorrain,[4] whom you may have heard of occasionally as a famous painter of classical landscapes. I don't exactly know (he has been dead so long) how many pictures he turned out, from first to last; but we will say, for the sake of argument, five hundred. Not five of these are offered for sale, perhaps, in the course of five years. Enlightened collectors of old pictures pour into the market by fifties, while genuine specimens of Claude, or of any other old master you like to mention, only dribble in by ones and twos. Under these circumstances, what is to be done? Are unoffending owners of galleries to be subjected to disappointment? Or are the works of Claude, and the other fellows, to be benevolently increased in number, to supply the wants of persons of taste and quality? No man of humanity but must lean to the latter alternative. The collectors, observe, don't know anything about it – they buy Claude (to take an instance from my own practice) as they buy all the other old masters, because of his reputation, not because of the pleasure they get from his works.

'Give them a picture with a good large ruin, fancy trees, prancing nymphs, and a watery sky; dirty it down dexterously to the right pitch; put it in an old frame; call it a Claude; and the sphere of the old master is enlarged, the collector is delighted, the picture-dealer is enriched, and the neglected modern artist claps a joyful hand on a well-filled pocket. Some men have a knack at making Rembrandts, others have a turn for Raphaels, Titians, Cuyps, Watteaus, and the rest of them.[5] Anyhow, we are all made happy – all pleased with each other – all benefited alike. Kindness is propagated and money is dispersed. Come along, my boy, and make an old master!'

V

He led the way into the street as he spoke. I felt the irresistible force of his logic. I sympathised with the ardent philanthropy of his motives. I burned with a noble ambition to extend the sphere of the old masters. In short, I took the tide at the flood, and followed Dick.

We plunged into some by-streets, struck off sharp into a court, and entered a house by a back door. A little old gentleman in a black velvet dressing gown met us in the passage. Dick instantly presented me: 'Mr Frank Softly – Mr Ishmael Pickup'. The little old gentleman stared at me distrustfully. I bowed to him with that inexorable politeness that I first learned under the instructive fist of Gentleman Jones, and which no force of adverse circumstances has ever availed to mitigate in after life. Mr Ishmael Pickup followed my lead. There is not the least need to describe him – he was a Jew.

'Go into the front showroom, and look at the pictures, while I speak to Mr Pickup,' said Dick, familiarly throwing open a door, and pushing me into a kind of gallery beyond. I found myself quite alone, surrounded by modern-antique pictures of all schools and sizes, of all degrees of dirt and dullness, with all the names of all the famous old masters, from Titian to Teniers, inscribed on their frames.[6] A 'pearly little gem', by Claude, with a ticket marked 'Sold' stuck into the frame, particularly attracted my attention. It was Dick's last ten-pound job, and it did credit to the youthful master's abilities as a workman-like maker of Claudes.

I have been informed that, since the time of which I am writing, the business of gentlemen of Mr Pickup's class has rather fallen off, and that there are dealers in pictures, now-adays, who are as just and honourable men as can be found in any profession or calling, anywhere under the sun. This change, which I report with sincerity and reflect on with amazement, is, as I suspect, mainly the result of certain whole-sale modern improvements in the position of contemporary art, which have necessitated improvements and alterations in the business of picture-dealing.

In my time, the encouragers of modern painting were limited in number to a few noblemen and gentlemen of ancient lineage, who, in matters of taste, at least, never presumed to think for themselves. They either inherited or bought a gallery more or less full of old pictures. It was as much a part of their education to put their faith in these on hearsay evidence, as to put their faith in King, Lords and Commons. It was an article of their creed to believe that the dead painters were the great men, and that the more the living painters imitated the dead, the better was their chance of becoming at some future day, and in a minor degree, great also. At certain times and seasons, these noblemen and gentlemen self-distrustfully strayed into the painting room of a modern artist, self-distrustfully allowed themselves to be rather attracted by his pictures, self-distrustfully bought one or two of them at prices that would appear so incredibly low, in these days, that I really cannot venture to quote them. The picture was sent home; the nobleman or gentleman (almost always an amiable and a hospitable man) would ask the artist to his house and introduce him to the distinguished individuals who frequented it, but would never admit his picture, on terms of equality, into the society even of the second-rate old masters. His work was hung up in any out-of-the-way corner of the gallery that could be found; it had been bought under protest; it was admitted by sufferance; its freshness and brightness damaged it terribly by contrast with the dirtiness and the dinginess of its elderly predecessors; and its only points selected for praise were those in which it most nearly resembled the peculiar mannerism of some old master, not those in which it resembled the characteristics of the old mistress – Nature.

The unfortunate artist had no court of appeal that he could turn to. Nobody beneath the nobleman, or the gentleman of ancient lineage, so much as thought of buying a modern picture. Nobody dared to whisper that the art of painting had in anywise been improved or worthily enlarged in its sphere by any modern professors. For one nobleman who was ready to buy one genuine modern picture at a small price, there were twenty noblemen ready to buy twenty more than doubtful old pictures at great prices. The consequence was that some of the most famous artists of the English school, whose pictures are now bought at auction sales for fabulous sums, were then hardly able to make an income. They were a scrupulously patient and conscientious body of men, who would as soon have thought of breaking into a house, or equalising the distribution of wealth, on the highway, by the simple machinery of a horse and pistol, as of making old masters to order. They sat resignedly in their lonely studios, surrounded by unsold pictures that have since been covered again and again with gold and banknotes by eager buyers at auctions and showrooms, whose money has gone into other than the painter's pockets – who have never dreamed that the painter had the smallest moral right to a farthing of it. Year after year, these martyrs of the brush stood, palette in hand, fighting the old battle of individual merit against contemporary dullness – fighting bravely, patiently, independently; and leaving to Mr Pickup and his pupils a complete monopoly of all the profit that could be extracted, in their line of business, from the feebly buttoned pocket of the patron, and the inexhaustible credulity of the connoisseur.

Now all this is changed. Traders and makers of all kinds of commodities have effected a revolution in the picture-world, never dreamt of by the noblemen and gentlemen of ancient lineage, and consistently protested against to this day by the very few of them who still remain alive.

The daring innovators started with the new notion of buying a picture that they themselves could admire and appreciate, and for the genuineness of which the artist was still living to vouch. These rough and ready customers were not to be led by rules or frightened by precedents; they were not to be easily imposed upon, for the article they wanted was not to be easily counterfeited. Sturdily holding to their own opinions, they thought incessant repetitions of saints, martyrs and holy families monotonous and uninteresting – and said so. They thought little pictures of ugly Dutch women scouring pots and drunken Dutchmen playing cards dirty and dear at the price – and said so. They saw that trees were green in nature and brown in the old masters, and they thought the latter colour not an improvement on the former – and said so. They wanted interesting subjects, variety, resemblance to nature, genuineness of the article, and fresh paint; they had no ancestors whose feelings, as founders of galleries, it was necessary to consult; no critical gentlemen and writers of valuable works to snub them when they were in spirits; nothing to lead them by the nose but their own shrewdness, their own interests, and their own tastes – so they turned their backs valiantly on the old masters, and marched off in a body to the living men.

From that time good modern pictures have risen in the scale. Even as articles of commerce and safe investments for money, they have now (as some disinterested collectors who dine at certain annual dinners I know of can testify) distanced the old pictures in the race. The modern painters who have survived the brunt of the battle have lived to see pictures for which they once asked hundreds selling for thousands, and the young generation making incomes by the brush in one year, which it would have cost the old heroes of the easel ten to accumulate. The posterity of Mr Pickup still do a tolerable stroke of business (making bright modern masters for the market that is glutted with the dingy old material), and will, probably, continue to thrive and multiply in the future: the one venerable institution of this world that we can safely count upon as likely to last being the institution of human folly. Nevertheless, if a wise man of the reformed taste wants a modern picture, there are places for him to go to now where he may be sure of getting it genuine; where, if the artist is not alive to vouch for his work, the facts at any rate have not had time to die that vouch for the dealer who sells it. In my time matters were rather different. The painters *we* throve by had died long enough ago for pedigrees to get confused and identities disputable; and if I had been desirous of really purchasing a genuine old master for myself – speaking as a practical man – I don't know where I should have gone to ask for one, or whose judgment I could have safely relied on to guard me from being cheated, before I bought it.

We are stopping a long time in the picture gallery, you will say. I am very sorry – but we must stay a little longer, for the sake of a living picture, the gem of the collection.

I was still admiring Mr Pickup's old masters, when a dirty little boy opened the door of the gallery, and introduced a young lady.

My heart – fancy my having a heart! – gave one great bound in me. I recognised the charming person whom I had followed in the street.

Her veil was not down this time. All the beauty of her large, soft, melancholy, brown eyes beamed on me. Her delicate complexion became suddenly suffused with a lovely rosy flush. Her glorious black hair – no! I will make an effort, I will suppress my ecstasies. Let me only say that she evidently recognised me. Will you believe it? – I felt myself colouring as I bowed to her. I never blushed before in my life. What a very curious sensation it is!

The horrid boy claimed her attention with a grin.

'Master's engaged,' he said. 'Please to wait here.'

'I don't wish to disturb Mr Pickup,' she answered.

What a voice! No! I am drifting back into ecstasies: her voice was worthy of her – I say no more.

'If you will be so kind as to show him this,' she proceeded. 'He knows what it is. And please say, my father is very ill and very anxious. It will be quite enough if Mr Pickup will only send me word by you – yes or no.'

She gave the boy an oblong slip of stamped paper. Evidently a promissory note. An angel on earth, sent by an inhuman father, to ask a Jew for discount! Monstrous!

The boy disappeared with the message.

I seized my opportunity of speaking to her. Don't ask me what I said! Never before (or since) have I talked such utter nonsense with such intense earnestness of purpose and such immeasurable depth of feeling. Do pray remember what you said yourself, the first time you had the chance of opening your heart to *your* young lady. The boy returned before I had half done, and gave her back the odious document.

'Mr Pickup's very sorry, miss. The answer is, no.'

She lost all her lovely colour, and sighed, and turned away. As she pulled down her veil, I saw the tears in her eyes. Did that piteous spectacle partially deprive me of my senses? I actually entreated her to let me be of some use – as if I had been an old friend, with money enough in my pocket to discount the note myself. She brought me back to my senses with the utmost gentleness.

'I am afraid you forget, sir, that we are strangers. Good morning.'

I followed her to the door. I asked leave to call on her father, and satisfy him about myself and my family connections. She only answered that her father was too ill to see visitors. I went out with her on to the landing. She turned on me sharply for the first time.

'You can see for yourself, sir, that I am in great distress. I appeal to you, as a gentleman, to spare me.'

If you still doubt whether I was really in love, let the facts speak for themselves. I hung my head, and let her go.

When I returned alone to the picture gallery – when I remembered that I had not even had the wit to improve my opportunity by discovering her name and address – I did really and seriously ask myself if these were the first symptoms of softening of the brain. I got up, and sat down again. I, the most audacious man of my age in London, had behaved like a bashful boy! Once more I had lost her – and this time, also, I had nobody but myself to blame for it.

These melancholy meditations were interrupted by the appearance of my friend, the artist, in the picture gallery. He approached me confidentially, and spoke in a mysterious whisper.

'Pickup is suspicious,' he said 'and I have had all the difficulty in the world to pave your way smoothly for you at the outset. However, if you can contrive to make a small Rembrandt, as a specimen, you may consider yourself employed here until further notice. I am obliged to particularise Rembrandt, because he is the only old master disengaged at present. The professional gentleman who used to do him died the other day in the Fleet – he had a turn for Rembrandts, and can't be easily replaced. Do you think you could step into his shoes? It's a peculiar gift, like an ear for music, or a turn for mathematics. Of course you will be put up to the simple elementary rules, and will have the professional gentleman's last Rembrandt as a guide; the rest depends, my dear friend, on your powers of imitation. Don't be discouraged by failures, but try again and again; and mind you are dirty and dark enough. You have heard a great deal about the light and shade of Rembrandt – remember always that, in your case, light means dusky yellow, and shade dense black; remember that, and – '

'No pay,' said the voice of Mr Pickup behind me; 'no pay, my dear, unlesh your Rembrandt ish good enough to take me in – even me, Ishmael, who dealsh in pictersh and knowsh what'sh what.'

What did I care about Rembrandt at that moment? I was thinking of my lost young lady and I should probably have taken no notice of Mr Pickup, if it had not occurred to me that the old wretch must know her father's name and address. I at once put the question. The Jew grinned, and shook his grisly head. 'Her father'sh in difficultiesh, and mum's the word, my dear.' To that answer he adhered, in spite of all that I could say to him.

With equal obstinacy I determined, sooner or later, to get my information.

I took service under Mr Pickup, purposing to make myself essential to his prosperity, in a commercial sense – and then to threaten him with offering my services to a rival manufacturer of old masters, unless he trusted me with the secret of the name and address. My plan looked promising enough at the time. But, as some wise person has said, man is the sport of circumstances. Mr Pickup and I parted company unexpectedly, on compulsion. And, of all the people in the world, my grandmother, Lady Malkinshaw, was the unconscious first cause of the events that brought me and the beloved object together again, for the third time!

VI

On the next day I was introduced to the Jew's workshop, and to the eminent gentlemen occupying it. My model Rembrandt was put before me, the simple elementary rules were explained, and my materials were all placed under my hands.

Regard for the lovers of the old masters, and for the moral well-being of society, forbids me to be particular about the nature of my labours, or to go into dangerous detail on the subject of my first failures and my subsequent success. I may, however, harmlessly admit that my Rembrandt was to be of the small or cabinet size, and that, as there was a run on burgomasters just then, my subject was naturally to be of the burgomaster sort. Three parts of my picture consisted entirely of different shades of dirty brown and black, the fourth being composed of a ray of yellow light falling upon the wrinkled face of a treacle-coloured old man. A dim glimpse of a hand, and a faint suggestion of something like a brass wash-hand-basin, completed the job, which gave great satisfaction to Mr Pickup, and which was described in the catalogue as –

> *A Burgomaster at Breakfast.* Originally in the collection of Mynheer Van Grubb, Amsterdam. A rare example of the master. Not engraved. The chiaroscuro in this extra-ordinary work is of a truly sublime character. Price, Two Hundred Guineas.

I got five pounds for it. I suppose Mr Pickup got one-ninety-five.

This was perhaps not very encouraging as a beginning, in a pecuniary point of view. But I was to get five pounds more, if my Rembrandt sold within a given time. It sold a week after it was in a fit state to be trusted in the showroom. I got my money, and began enthusiastically on another Rembrandt – *A Burgomaster's Wife Poking the Fire*. Last time, the chiaroscuro of the master had been yellow and black; this time it was to be red and black. I was just on the point of forcing my way into Mr Pickup's confidence, as I had resolved, when a catastrophe happened, which shut up the shop and abruptly terminated my experience as a maker of old masters.

The Burgomaster's Breakfast had been sold to a new customer, a venerable connoisseur, blessed with a great fortune and a large picture gallery. The old gentleman was in raptures with the picture – with its tone, with its breadth, with its grand feeling for effect, with its simple treatment of detail. It wanted nothing, in his opinion, but a little cleaning. Mr Pickup knew the raw and ticklish state of the surface, however, far too well, to allow of even an attempt at performing this process, and solemnly asserted that he was acquainted with no cleansing preparation that could be used on the Rembrandt without danger of 'flaying off the last exquisite glazings of the immortal master's brush'. The old gentleman was quite satisfied with this reason for not cleaning the Burgomaster, and took away his purchase in his own carriage on the spot.

For three weeks we heard nothing more of him. At the end of that time, a Hebrew friend of Mr Pickup, employed in a lawyer's office, terrified us all by the information that a gentleman related to our venerable connoisseur had seen the Rembrandt, had pronounced it to be an impudent counterfeit, and had engaged on his own account to have the picture tested in a court of law, and to charge the seller and maker thereof with conspiring to obtain money under false pretences. Mr Pickup and I looked at each other with very blank faces on receiving this agreeable piece of news. What was to be done?

I recovered the full use of my faculties first, and I was the man who solved that important and difficult question, while the rest were still utterly bewildered by it. 'Will you promise me five and twenty pounds in the presence of these gentlemen if I get you out of this scrape?' said I to my terrified employer. Ishmael Pickup wrung his dirty hands and answered, 'Yesh, my dear!'

Our informant in this awkward matter was employed at the office of the lawyers who were to have the conducting of the case against us, and he was able to tell me some of the things I most wanted to know in relation to the picture.

I found out from him that the Rembrandt was still in our customer's possession. The old gentleman had consented to the question of its genuineness being tried, but had far too high an idea of his own knowledge as a connoisseur to incline to the opinion that he had been taken in. His suspicious relative was not staying in the house, but was in the habit of visiting him, every day, in the forenoon. That was as much as I wanted to know from others. The rest depended on myself, on luck, time, human credulity, and a smattering of chemical knowledge that I had acquired in the days of my medical studies. I left the conclave at the picture-dealer's forthwith, and purchased at the nearest druggist's a bottle containing a certain powerful liquid, which I decline to particularise on high moral grounds. I labelled the bottle 'The Amsterdam Cleansing Compound', and I wrapped round it the following note:

Mr Pickup's respectful compliments to Mr – (let us say, Green). Is rejoiced to state that he finds himself unexpectedly able to forward Mr Green's views relative to the cleaning of The Burgomaster's Breakfast. *The enclosed compound has just reached him from Amsterdam. It is made from a recipe found among the papers of Rembrandt himself – has been used with the most astonishing results on the Master's pictures in every gallery of Holland, and is now being applied to the surface of the largest Rembrandt in Mr P.'s own collection. Directions for use: Lay the picture flat, pour the whole contents of the bottle over it gently, so as to flood the entire surface; leave the liquid on the surface for six hours, then wipe it off briskly with a soft cloth of as large a size as can be conveniently used. The effect will be the most wonderful removal of all dirt, and a complete and brilliant metamorphosis of the present dingy surface of the picture.*

I left this note and the bottle myself at two o'clock that day, then went home, and confidently awaited the result.

The next morning our friend from the office called, announcing himself by a burst of laughter outside the door. Mr Green had implicitly followed the directions in the letter the moment he received it – had allowed the 'Amsterdam Cleansing Compound' to remain on the Rembrandt until eight o'clock in the evening – had called for the softest linen cloth in the whole house – and had then, with his own venerable hands, carefully wiped off the compound, and with it the whole surface of the picture! The brown, the black, the burgomaster, the breakfast, and the ray of yellow light, all came clean off together in considerably less than a minute of time. If the picture was brought into court now, the evidence it could give against us was limited to a bit of plain panel, and a mass of black pulp rolled up in a duster.

Our line of defence was, of course, that the compound had been improperly used. For the rest, we relied with well-placed confidence on the want of evidence against us. Mr Pickup wisely closed his shop for a while, and went off to the Continent to ransack the foreign galleries. I received my five and twenty pounds, rubbed out the beginning of my second Rembrandt, closed the back door of the workshop behind me, and there was another scene of my life at an end. I had but one circumstance to regret – and I did regret it bitterly. I was still as ignorant as ever of the young lady's name and address.

My first visit was to the studio of my excellent artist-friend, whom I have already presented to the reader under the sympathetic name of 'Dick'. He greeted me with a letter in his hand. It was addressed to me – it had been left at the studio a few days since, and (marvel of all marvels!) the handwriting was Mr Batterbury's. Had this philanthropic man not done befriending me even yet? Were there any present or prospective advantages to be got out of him still? Read his letter, and judge.

SIR – Although you have forfeited by your ungentlemanly conduct toward myself, and your heartlessly mischievous reception of my dear wife, all claim upon the forbearance of the most forbearing of your relatives, I am disposed, from motives of regard for the tranquillity of Mrs Batterbury's family, and of sheer good nature so far as I am myself concerned, to afford you one more chance of retrieving your position by leading a respectable life. The situation I am enabled to offer you is that of secretary to a new Literary and Scientific Institution, about to be opened in the town of Duskydale, near which neighbourhood I possess, as you must be aware, some landed property. The office has been placed at my disposal, as vice-president of the new Institution. The salary is fifty pounds a year, with apartments on the attic-floor of the building. The duties are various, and will be explained to you by the local committee, if you choose to present yourself to them with the enclosed letter of introduction. After the unscrupulous manner in which you have imposed on my liberality by deceiving me into giving you fifty pounds for an audacious caricature of myself, which it is impossible to hang up in any room of the house, I think this instance of my forgiving disposition still to befriend you, after all that has happened, ought to appeal to any better feelings that you may still have left, and revive the long dormant emotions of repentance and self-reproach, when you think on your obedient servant,

– DANIEL BATTERBURY

Bless me! What a long-winded style, and what a fuss about fifty pounds a year and a bed in an attic! These were naturally the first emotions that Mr Batterbury's letter produced in me. What was his real motive for writing it? I hope nobody will do me so great an injustice as to suppose that I hesitated for one instant about the way of finding *that* out. Of course I started off directly to enquire if Lady Malkinshaw had had another narrow escape of dying before me.

'Much better, sir,' answered my grandmother's venerable butler, wiping his lips carefully before he spoke; 'her ladyship's health has been much improved since her accident.'

'Accident!' I exclaimed. 'What, another? Lately? Stairs again?'

'No, sir; the drawing-room window this time,' answered the butler, with semi-tipsy gravity. 'Her ladyship's sight having been defective of late years occasions her some difficulty in calculating distances. Three days ago, her ladyship went to look out of the window, and, miscalculating the distance – '

Here the butler, with a fine dramatic feeling for telling a story, stopped just before the climax of the narrative, and looked me in the face with an expression of the deepest sympathy.

'And miscalculating the distance?' I repeated impatiently.

'Put her head through a pane of glass,' said the butler, in a soft voice suited to the pathetic nature of the communication. 'By great good fortune her ladyship had been dressed for the day, and had got her turban on. This saved her ladyship's head. But her ladyship's neck, sir, had a very narrow escape. A bit of the broken glass wounded it within half a quarter of an inch of the carotty artery' (meaning, probably, carotid); 'I heard the medical gentleman say, and shall never forget it to my dying day, that her ladyship's life had been saved by a hair's breadth. As it was, the blood lost (the medical gentleman said that, too, sir) was accidentally of the greatest possible benefit, being apoplectic, in the way of clearing out the system. Her ladyship's appetite has been improved ever since – the carriage is out airing of her at this very moment – likewise, she takes the footman's arm and the maid's up and downstairs now, which she never would hear of before this last accident. "I feel ten years younger" (those were her ladyship's own words to me, this very day), "I feel ten years younger, Vokins, since I broke the drawing-room window." And her ladyship looks it!'

No doubt. Here was the key to Mr Batterbury's letter of forgiveness. His chance of receiving the legacy looked now further off than ever; he could not feel the same confidence as his wife in my power of living down any amount of starvation and adversity; and he was, therefore, quite ready to take the first opportunity of promoting my precious personal welfare and security, of which he could avail himself, without spending a farthing of money. I saw it all clearly, and admired the hereditary toughness of the Malkinshaw family more gratefully than ever. What should I do? Go to Duskydale? Why not? It didn't matter to me where I went, now that I had no hope of ever seeing those lovely brown eyes again.

I got to my new destination the next day, presented my credentials, gave myself the full advantage of my high connections, and was received with enthusiasm and distinction.

I found the new Institution torn by internal schisms even before it was opened to the public. Two factions governed it – a grave faction and a gay faction. Two questions agitated it: the first referring to the propriety of celebrating the opening season by a public ball, and the second to the expediency of admitting novels into the library. The grim puritan interest of the whole neighbourhood was, of course, on the grave side – against both dancing and novels, as proposed by local loose thinkers and latitudinarians of every degree. I was officially introduced to the debate at the height of the squabble, and found myself one of a large party in a small room, sitting round a long table, each man of us with a new pewter inkstand, a new quill pen, and a clean sheet of foolscap paper before him. Seeing that everybody spoke, I got on my legs along with the rest, and made a slashing speech on the loose-thinking side. I was followed by the leader of the grim faction – an unlicked curate of the largest dimensions.

'If there were, so to speak, no other reason against dancing,' said my reverend opponent, 'there is one unanswerable objection to it. Gentlemen! John the Baptist lost his head through dancing!'[7]

Every man of the grim faction hammered delightedly on the table as that formidable argument was produced, and the curate sat down in triumph. I jumped up to reply, amid the counter-cheering of the loose-thinkers, but before I could say a word the president of the Institution and the rector of the parish came into the room.

They were both men of authority, men of sense, and fathers of charming daughters, and they turned the scale on the right side in no time. The question relating to the admission of novels was postponed, and the question of dancing or no dancing was put to the vote on the spot. The president, the rector and myself, the three handsomest and highest-bred men in the assembly, led the way on the liberal side, waggishly warning all gallant gentlemen present to beware of disappointing the young ladies. This decided the waverers, and the waverers decided the majority. My first business, as secretary, was the drawing out of a model card of admission to the ball.

My next occupation was to look at the rooms provided for me.

The Duskydale Institution occupied a badly repaired ten-roomed house, with a great flimsy saloon built at one side of it, smelling of paint and damp plaster, and called the Lecture Theatre. It was the chilliest, ugliest, emptiest, gloomiest place I ever entered in my life; the idea of doing anything but sitting down and crying in it seemed to me quite preposterous, but the committee took a different view of the matter, and praised the Lecture Theatre as a perfect ballroom. The secretary's apartments were two garrets, asserting themselves in the most barefaced manner, without an attempt at disguise. If I had intended to do more than earn my first quarter's salary, I should have complained. But as I had not the slightest intention of remaining at Duskydale, I could afford to establish a reputation for amiability by saying nothing.

'Have you seen Mr Softly, the new secretary? A most distinguished person, and quite an acquisition to the neighbourhood.' Such was the popular opinion of me among the young ladies and the liberal inhabitants. 'Have you seen Mr Softly, the new secretary? A worldly, vainglorious young man. The last person in England to promote the interests of our new Institution.' Such was the counter-estimate of me among the puritan population. I report both opinions quite disinterestedly. There is generally something to be said on either side of every question, and, as for me, I can always hold up the scales impartially, even when my own character is the substance weighing in them. Readers of ancient history need not be reminded, at this time of day, that there may be Roman virtue even in a Rogue.

The objects, interests, and general business of the Duskydale Institution were matters with which I never thought of troubling myself on assuming the duties of secretary. All my energies were given to the arrangements connected with the opening ball.

I was elected by acclamation to the office of general manager of the entertainments, and I did my best to deserve the confidence reposed in me, leaving literature and science, so far as I was concerned, perfectly at liberty to advance themselves or not, just as they liked. Whatever my colleagues may have done, after I left them, nobody at Duskydale can accuse me of having ever been accessory to the disturbing of quiet people with useful knowledge. I took the arduous and universally neglected duty of teaching the English people how to be amused entirely on my own shoulders, and left the easy and customary business of making them miserable to others.

My unhappy countrymen! (and thrice unhappy they of the poorer sort) – any man can preach to them, lecture to them, and form them into classes – but where is the man who can get them to amuse themselves? Anybody may cram their poor heads, but who will brighten their grave faces? Don't read story books, don't go to plays, don't dance! Finish your long day's work and then intoxicate your minds with solid history, revel in the too-attractive luxury of the lecture room, sink under the soft temptation of classes for mutual instruction! How many potent, grave and reverent tongues discourse to the popular ear in these siren strains, and how obediently and resignedly this same weary popular ear listens! What if a bold man spring up one day, crying aloud in our social wilderness, 'Play, for heaven's sake, or you will work yourselves into a nation of automatons! Shake a loose leg to a lively fiddle! Women of England! drag the lecturer off the rostrum, and the male mutual instructor out of the class, and ease their poor addled heads of evenings by making them dance and sing with you. Accept no offer from any man who cannot be proved, for a year past, to have systematically lost his dignity at least three times a week, after office hours. You, daughters of Eve, who have that wholesome love of pleasure that is one of the greatest adornments of the female character, set up a society for the promotion of universal amusement, and save the British nation from the lamentable social consequences of its own gravity!' Imagine a voice crying lustily after this fashion – what sort of echoes would it find? – Groans?

I know what sort of echoes my voice found. They were so discouraging to me, and to the frivolous minority of pleasure-seekers, that I recommended lowering the price of admission so as to suit the means of any decent people who were willing to leave off money-grubbing and tear themselves from the charms of mutual instruction for one evening at least. The proposition was indignantly negatived by the managers of the Institution. I am so singularly obstinate a man that I was not to be depressed even by this.

My next efforts to fill the ballroom could not be blamed. I procured a local directory, put fifty tickets in my pocket, dressed myself in nankeen pantaloons and a sky-blue coat (then the height of fashion), and set forth to tout for dancers among all the members of the genteel population, who, not being notorious puritans, had also not been so obliging as to take tickets for the ball. There never was any pride or bashfulness about me. Excepting certain periods of suspense and anxiety, I am as even-tempered a Rogue as you have met with anywhere since the days of Gil Blas.[8]

My temperament being opposed to doing anything with regularity, I opened the directory at hazard, and determined to make my first call at the first house that caught my eye. Vallombrosa Vale Cottages. No. 1. Doctor and Miss Dulcifer. Very good. I have no preferences. Let me sell the first two tickets there. I found the place; I opened the garden gate; I advanced to the door, innocently wondering what sort of people I should find inside.

If I am asked what was the true reason for this extraordinary activity on my part, in serving the interests of a set of people for whom I cared nothing, I must honestly own that the loss of my young lady was at the bottom of it. Any occupation was welcome that kept my mind, in some degree at least, from dwelling on the bitter disappointment that had befallen me. When I rang the bell at no. 1, did I feel no presentiment of the exquisite surprise in store for me? I felt nothing of the sort. The fact is, my digestion is excellent. Presentiments are more closely connected than is generally supposed with a weak state of stomach.

I asked for Miss Dulcifer, and was shown into the sitting room.

Don't expect me to describe my sensations: hundreds of sensations flew all over me. There she was, sitting alone, near the window! There she was, with nimble white fingers, working a silk purse!

The melancholy in her face and manner, when I had last seen her, appeared no more. She was prettily dressed in maize colour, and the room was well furnished. Her father had evidently got over his difficulties. I had been inclined to laugh at his odd name, when I found it in the directory! Now I began to dislike it, because it was her name, too. It was a consolation to remember that she could change it. Would she change it for mine?

I was the first to recover; I boldly drew a chair near her and took her hand.

'You see,' I said, 'it is of no use to try to avoid me. This is the third time we have met. Will you receive me as a visitor, under these extraordinary circumstances? Will you give me a little happiness to compensate for what I have suffered since you left me?'

She smiled and blushed.

'I am so surprised,' she answered, 'I don't know what to say.'

'Disagreeably surprised?' I asked.

She first went on with her work, and then replied (a little sadly, as I thought), 'No!'

I was ready enough to take advantage of my opportunities this time, but she contrived with perfect politeness to stop me. She seemed to remember with shame, poor soul, the circumstances under which I had last seen her.

'How do you come to be at Duskydale?' she enquired, abruptly changing the subject. 'And how did you find us out here?'

While I was giving her the necessary explanations her father came in. I looked at him with considerable curiosity.

A tall, stout gentleman with impressive respectability oozing out of him at every pore – with a swelling outline of black-waistcoated stomach, with a lofty forehead, with a smooth double chin resting pulpily on a white cravat. Everything in harmony about him except his eyes, and these were so sharp, bright and resolute that they seemed to contradict the bland conventionality that overspread all the rest of the man. Eyes with wonderful intelligence and self-dependence in them; perhaps, also, with something a little false in them, which I might have discovered immediately under ordinary circumstances, but I looked at the doctor through the medium of his daughter, and saw nothing of him at the first glance but his merits.

'We are both very much indebted to you, sir, for your politeness in calling,' he said, with excessive civility of manner. 'But our stay at this place has drawn to an end. I only came here for the re-establishment of my daughter's health. She has benefited greatly by the change of air, and we have arranged to return home tomorrow. Otherwise, we should have gladly profited by your kind offer of tickets for the ball.'

Of course I had one eye on the young lady while he was speaking. She was looking at her father, and a sudden sadness was stealing over her face. What did it mean? Disappointment at missing the ball? No, it was a much deeper feeling than that. My interest was excited. I addressed a complimentary entreaty to the doctor not to take his daughter away from us. I asked him to reflect on the irreparable eclipse that he would be casting over the Duskydale ballroom. To my amazement, she only looked down gloomily on her work while I spoke; her father laughed contemptuously.

'We are too completely strangers here,' he said, 'for our loss to be felt by any one. From all that I can gather, society in Duskydale will be glad to hear of our departure. I beg your pardon, Alicia – I ought to have said *my* departure.'

Her name was Alicia! I declare it was a luxury to me to hear it – the name was so appropriate, so suggestive of the grace and dignity of her beauty.

I turned toward her when the doctor had done. She looked more gloomily than before. I protested against the doctor's account of himself. He laughed again, with a quick distrustful look, this time, at his daughter.

'If you were to mention my name among your respectable inhabitants,' he went on, with a strong, sneering emphasis on the word respectable, 'they would most likely purse up their lips and look grave at it. Since I gave up practice as a physician, I have engaged in chemical investigations on a large scale, destined, I hope, to lead to some important public results. Until I arrive at these, I am necessarily obliged, in my own interests, to keep my experiments secret, and to impose similar discretion on the workmen whom I employ. This unavoidable appearance of mystery, and the strictly retired life that my studies compel me to lead, offend the narrow-minded people in my part of the county, close to Barkingham, and the unpopularity of my pursuits has followed me here. The general opinion, I believe, is, that I am seeking by unholy arts for the philosopher's stone. Plain man, as you see me, I find myself getting quite the reputation of a Doctor Faustus in the popular mind. Even educated people in this very place shake their heads and pity my daughter there for living with an alchemical parent, within easy smelling-distance of an explosive laboratory. Excessively absurd, is it not?'

It might have been excessively absurd, but the lovely Alicia sat with her eyes on her work, looking as if it were excessively sad, and not giving her father the faintest answering smile when he glanced toward her and laughed, as he said his last words. I could not at all tell what to make of it. The doctor talked of the social consequences of his chemical enquiries as if he were living in the middle ages. However, I was far too anxious to see the charming brown eyes again to ask questions that would be sure to keep them cast down. So I changed the topic to chemistry in general and, to the doctor's evident astonishment and pleasure, told him of my own early studies in the science.

This led to the mention of my father, whose reputation had reached the ears of Dr Dulcifer. As he told me that, his daughter looked up – the sun of beauty shone on me again! I touched next on my high connections, and on Lady Malkinshaw; I described myself as temporarily banished from home for humorous caricaturing and amiable youthful wildness. She was interested; she smiled – and the sun of beauty shone warmer than ever! I diverged to general topics, and got brilliant and amusing. She laughed – the nightingale notes of her merriment bubbled into my ears caressingly – why could I not shut my eyes and listen to them? Her colour rose; her face grew animated. Poor soul! A little lively company was but too evidently a rare treat to her. Under such circumstances, who would not be amusing? If she had said to me, 'Mr Softly, I like tumbling,' I should have made a clown of myself on the spot. I should have stood on my head (if I could), and been amply rewarded for the graceful exertion, if the eyes of Alicia had looked kindly on my elevated heels!

How long I stayed is more than I can tell. Lunch came up. I ate and drank, and grew more amusing than ever. When I at last rose to go, the brown eyes looked on me very kindly, and the doctor gave me his card.

'If you don't mind trusting yourself in the clutches of Doctor Faustus,' he said, with a gay smile, 'I shall be delighted to see you if you are ever in the neighbourhood of Barkingham.'

I wrung his hand, mentally relinquishing my secretaryship while I thanked him for the invitation. I put out my hand next to his daughter, and the dear friendly girl met the advance with the most charming readiness. She gave me a good, hearty, vigorous, uncompromising shake. O precious right hand! never did I properly appreciate your value until that moment.

Going out with my head in the air, and my senses in the seventh heaven, I jostled an elderly gentleman passing before the garden gate. I turned round to apologise; it was my brother in office, the estimable treasurer of the Duskydale Institute.

'I have been half over the town looking after you,' he said. 'The managing committee, on reflection, consider your plan of personally soliciting public attendance at the hall to be compromising the dignity of the Institution, and beg you, therefore, to abandon it.'

'Very well,' said I, 'there is no harm done. Thus far, I have only solicited two persons, Dr and Miss Dulcifer, in that delightful little cottage there.'

'You don't mean to say you have asked *them* to come to the ball!'

'To be sure I have. And I am sorry to say they can't accept the invitation. Why should they not be asked?'

'Because nobody visits them.'

'And why should nobody visit them?'

The treasurer put his arm confidentially through mine, and walked me on a few steps.

'In the first place,' he said, 'Dr Dulcifer's name is not down in the Medical List.'

'Some mistake,' I suggested, in my offhand way. 'Or some foreign doctor's degree not recognised by the prejudiced people in England.'

'In the second place,' continued the treasurer, 'we have found out that he is not visited at Barkingham. Consequently, it would be the height of imprudence to visit him here.'

'Pooh! pooh! All the nonsense of narrow-minded people, because he lives a retired life, and is engaged in finding out chemical secrets that the ignorant public don't know how to appreciate.'

'The shutters are always up in the front top windows of his house at Barkingham,' said the treasurer, lowering his voice mysteriously. 'I know it from a friend resident near him. The windows themselves are barred. It is currently reported that the top of the house, inside, is shut off by iron doors from the bottom. Workmen are employed there who don't belong to the neighbourhood, who don't drink at the public houses, who only associate with each other. Unfamiliar smells and noises find their way outside sometimes. Nobody in the house can be got to talk. The doctor, as he calls himself, does not even make an attempt to get into society, does not even try to see company for the sake of his poor unfortunate daughter. What do you think of all that?'

'Think!' I repeated contemptuously. 'I think the inhabitants of Barkingham are the best finders of mare's nests in all England. The doctor is making important chemical discoveries (the possible value of which I can appreciate, being chemical myself), and he is not quite fool enough to expose valuable secrets to the view of all the world. His laboratory is at the top of the house, and he wisely shuts it off from the bottom to prevent accidents. He is one of the best fellows I ever met with, and his daughter is the loveliest girl in the world. What do you all mean by making mysteries about nothing? He has given me an invitation to go and see him. I suppose the next thing you will find out is that there is something underhand even in that?'

'You won't accept the invitation?'

'I shall, at the very first opportunity; and if you had seen Miss Alicia, so would you.'

'Don't go. Take my advice and don't go,' said the treasurer, gravely. 'You are a young man. Reputable friends are of importance to you at the outset of life. I say nothing against Dr Dulcifer – he came here as a stranger, and he goes away again as a stranger – but you can't be sure that his purpose in asking you so readily to his house is a harmless one. Making a new acquaintance is always a doubtful speculation, but when a man is not visited by his respectable neighbours – '

'Because he doesn't open his shutters,' I interposed sarcastically.

'Because there are doubts about him and his house that he will not clear up,' retorted the treasurer. 'You can take your own way. You may turn out right, and we may all be wrong; I can only say again, it is rash to make doubtful acquaintances. Sooner or later you are always sure to repent it. In your place I should certainly not accept the invitation.'

'In my place, my dear sir,' I answered, 'you would do exactly what I mean to do.'

The treasurer took his arm out of mine, and without saying another word, wished me good morning.

VII

I had spoken confidently enough while arguing the question of Dr Dulcifer's respectability with the treasurer of the Duskydale Institution; but, if my perceptions had not been blinded by my enthusiastic admiration for Alicia, I think I should have secretly distrusted my own opinion as soon as I was left by myself. Had I been in full possession of my senses, I might have questioned, on reflection, whether the doctor's method of accounting for the suspicions that kept his neighbours aloof from him was quite satisfactory. Love is generally described, I believe, as the tender passion. When I remember the insidiously relaxing effect of it on all my faculties, I feel inclined to alter the popular definition and to call it a moral vapour-bath.

What the managing committee of the Duskydale Institution thought of the change in me, I cannot imagine. The doctor and his daughter left the town on the day they had originally appointed, before I could make any excuse for calling again; and, as a necessary consequence of their departure, I lost all interest in the affairs of the ball, and yawned in the faces of the committee when I was obliged to be present at their deliberations in my official capacity.

It was all Alicia with me, whatever they did. I read the minutes through a soft medium of maize-coloured skirts. Notes of melodious laughter bubbled, in my mind's ear, through all the drawling and stammering of our speech-making members. When our dignified president thought he had caught my eye, and made oratorical overtures to me from the top of the table, I was lost in the contemplation of silk purses and white fingers weaving them. I meant 'Alicia' when I said 'hear, hear' – and when I officially produced my subscription list, it was all aglow with the roseate hues of the marriage-licence. If any unsympathetic male readers should think this statement exaggerated, I appeal to the ladies – *they* will appreciate the rigid, yet tender, truth of it.

The night of the ball came. I have nothing but the vaguest recollection of it.

I remember that the more the perverse lecture theatre was warmed the more persistently it smelled of damp plaster, and that the more brightly it was lighted, the more overgrown and lonesome it looked. I can recall to mind that the company assembled numbered about fifty, the room being big enough to hold three hundred. I have a vision still before me of twenty out of these fifty guests, solemnly executing intricate figure-dances, under the superintendence of an infirm local dancing-master – a mere speck of fidgety human wretchedness twisting about in the middle of an empty floor. I see, faintly, down the dim vista of the past, an agreeable figure, like myself, with a cocked hat under its arm, black tights on its lightly tripping legs, a rosette in its buttonhole, and an engaging smile on its face, walking from end to end of the room, in the character of master of the ceremonies. These visions and events I can recall vaguely and with them my remembrances of the ball come to a close. It was a complete failure, and that would, of itself, have been enough to sicken me of remaining at the Duskydale Institution, even if I had not had any reasons of the tender sort for wishing to extend my travels in rural England to the neighbourhood of Barkingham.

The difficulty was how to find a decent pretext for getting away. Fortunately, the managing committee relieved me of any perplexity on this head, by passing a resolution, one day, which called upon the president to remonstrate with me on my want of proper interest in the affairs of the Institution.

I replied to the remonstrance that the affairs of the Institution were so hopelessly dull that it was equally absurd and unjust to expect any human being to take the smallest interest in them. At this there arose an indignant cry of 'Resign!' from the whole committee, to which I answered politely, that I should be delighted to oblige the gentlemen, and to go forthwith, on condition of receiving a quarter's salary in the way of previous compensation.

After a sordid opposition from an economical minority, my condition of departure was accepted. I wrote a letter of resignation, received in exchange twelve pounds ten shillings, and took my place, that same day, on the box-seat of the Barkingham mail.

Rather changeable this life of mine, was it not? Before I was twenty-five years of age, I had tried doctoring, caricaturing, portrait-painting, old picture-making, and Institution-managing; and now, with the help of Alicia, I was about to try how a little marrying would suit me. Surely, Shakespeare must have had me prophetically in his eye, when he wrote about 'one man in his time playing many parts'. What a character I should have made for him, if he had only been alive now!

I found out from the coachman, among other matters, that there was a famous fishing-stream near Barkingham, and the first thing I did, on arriving at the town, was to buy a rod and line.

It struck me that my safest way of introducing myself would be to tell Dr Dulcifer that I had come to the neighbourhood for a little fishing, and so to prevent him from fancying that I was suspiciously prompt in availing myself of his offered hospitality. I put up, of course, at the inn – stuck a large parchment book of flies half in and half out of the pocket of my shooting-jacket – and set off at once to the doctor's. The waiter of whom I asked my way stared distrustfully while he directed me. The people at the inn had evidently heard of my new friend, and were not favourably disposed toward the cause of scientific investigation.

The house stood about a mile out of the town, in a dip of ground near the famous fishing-stream. It was a lonely, old-fashioned red-brick building, surrounded by high walls, with a garden and plantation behind it.

As I rang at the gate-bell, I looked up at the house. Sure enough all the top windows in front were closed with shutters and barred. I was let in by a man in livery, who, however, in manners and appearance looked much more like a workman in disguise than a footman. He had a very suspicious eye, and he fixed it on me unpleasantly when I handed him my card.

I was shown into a morning room exactly like other morning rooms in country houses.

After a long delay the doctor came in, with scientific butchers' sleeves on his arms, and an apron tied round his portly waist. He apologised for coming down in his working dress, and said everything that was civil and proper about the pleasure of unexpectedly seeing me again so soon. There was something rather preoccupied, I thought, in those brightly resolute eyes of his, but I naturally attributed it to the engrossing influence of his scientific enquiries. He was evidently not at all taken in by my story about coming to Barkingham to fish, but he saw, as well as I did, that it would do to keep up appearances, and contrived to look highly interested immediately in my parchment book. I asked after his daughter. He said she was in the garden, and proposed that we should go and find her. We did find her, with a pair of scissors in her hand, out-blooming the flowers that she was trimming. She looked really glad to see me – her brown eyes beamed clear and kindly – she gave my hand another inestimable shake – the summer breezes waved her black curls gently upward from her waist – she had on a straw hat and a brown Holland gardening dress. I eyed it with all the practical interest of a linen draper. O Brown Holland you are but a coarse and cheap fabric, yet how soft and priceless you look when clothing the figure of Alicia!

I lunched with them. The doctor recurred to the subject of my angling intentions, and asked his daughter if she had heard what parts of the stream at Barkingham were best for fishing in.

She replied, with a mixture of modest evasiveness and adorable simplicity, that she had sometimes seen gentlemen angling from a meadow-bank about a quarter of a mile below her flower garden. I risked everything in my usual venturesome way, and asked if she would show me where the place was, in case I called the next morning with my fishing rod. She looked dutifully at her father. He smiled and nodded. Inestimable parent!

On rising to take leave, I was rather curious to know whether he would offer me a bed in the house, or not. He detected the direction of my thoughts in my face and manner, and apologised for not having a bed to offer me, every spare room in the house being occupied by his chemical assistants and by the lumber of laboratories. Even while he was speaking those few words, Alicia's face changed just as I had seen it change at our first interview. The downcast, gloomy expression overspread it again. Her father's eye wandered toward her when mine did, and suddenly assumed the same distrustful look that I remembered detecting in it, under similar circumstances, at Duskydale. What could this mean?

The doctor shook hands with me in the hall, leaving the workman-like footman to open the door.

I stopped to admire a fine pair of stag's antlers. The footman coughed impatiently. I still lingered, hearing the doctor's foot-steps ascending the stairs. They suddenly stopped, and then there was a low heavy clang, like the sound of a closing door made of iron, or of some other unusually strong material; then total silence, interrupted by another impatient cough from the workman-like footman. After that, I thought my wisest pro-ceeding would be to go away before my mysterious attendant was driven to practical extremities.

Between thoughts of Alicia, and inquisitive yearnings to know more about the doctor's experiments, I passed rather a restless night at my inn.

The next morning, I found the lovely mistress of my destiny, with the softest of shawls on her shoulders, the brightest of parasols in her hand, and the smart little straw hat of the day before on her head, ready to show me the way to the fishing place. If I could be sure beforehand that these pages would only be read by persons actually occupied in the making of love – that oldest and longest-established of all branches of manu-facturing industry – I could go into some very tender and interesting particulars on the subject of my first day's fishing, under the adorable auspices of Alicia. But as I cannot hope for a wholly sympathetic audience – as there may be monks, misogynists, political economists, and other professedly hard-hearted persons present among those whom I now address – I think it best to keep to safe generalities, and to describe my love-making in as few sentences as the vast, though soft, importance of the subject will allow me to use.

Let me confess, then, that I assumed the character of a fastidious angler, and managed to be a week in discovering the right place to fish in – always, it is unnecessary to say, under Alicia's guidance. We went up the stream and down the stream, on one side. We crossed the bridge, and went up the stream and down the stream on the other. We got into a punt and went up the stream (with great difficulty), and down the stream (with great ease). We landed on a little island, and walked all round it, and inspected the stream attentively from a central point of view. We found the island damp and went back to the bank, and up the stream, and over the bridge, and down the stream again; and then, for the first time, the sweet girl turned appealingly to me, and confessed that she had exhausted her artless knowledge of the locality. It was exactly a week from the day when I had first followed her into the fields with my fishing rod over my shoulder, and I had never yet caught anything but Alicia's hand, and that not with my hook.

We sat down close together on the bank, entirely in consequence of our despair at not finding a good fishing place. I looked at the brown eyes, and they turned away observantly down the stream. I followed them, and they turned away enquiringly up the stream. Was this angel of patience and kindness still looking for a fishing place? And was it *up* the stream, after all? No! – she smiled and shook her head when I asked the question, and the brown eyes suddenly stole a look at me. I could hold out no longer. In one breathless moment I caught hold of both her hands – in one stammering sentence I asked her if she would be my wife.

She tried faintly to free her hands – gave up the attempt – smiled – made an effort to look grave – gave that up, too – sighed suddenly – checked herself suddenly – said nothing. Perhaps I ought to have taken my answer for granted, but the least businesslike man that ever lived becomes an eminently practical character in matters of love. I repeated my question. She looked away confusedly; her eye lighted on a corner of her father's red-brick house, peeping through a gap in the plantation already mentioned, and her blushing cheeks lost their colour instantly. I felt her hands grow cold; she drew them resolutely out of mine, and rose with the tears in her eyes. Had I offended her?

'No,' she said when I asked her the question, and turned to me again, and held out her hand with such frank, fearless kindness that I almost fell on my knees to thank her for it.

Might I hope ever to hear her say 'Yes' to the question that I had asked on the riverbank?

She sighed bitterly, and turned again toward the red-brick house.

Was there any family reason against her saying 'Yes'? Anything that I must not enquire into? Any opposition to be dreaded from her father?

The moment I mentioned her father, she shrank away from me and burst into a violent fit of crying.

'Don't speak of it again!' she said in a broken voice. 'I mustn't – you mustn't – ah, don't, don't say a word more about it! I'm not distressed with you – it is not your fault. Don't say anything – leave me quiet for a minute. I shall soon be better if you leave me quiet.'

She dried her eyes directly, with a shiver as if it was cold, and took my arm. I led her back to the house-gate, and then, feeling that I could not go in to lunch as usual, after what had happened, said I would return to the fishing place.

'Shall I come to dinner this evening?' I asked, as I rang the gate-bell for her.

'Oh, yes – yes! – do come, or he – '

The mysterious manservant opened the door, and we parted before she could say the next words.

VIII

I went back to the fishing place with a heavy heart, overcome by mournful thoughts for the first time in my life. It was plain that she did not dislike me, and equally plain that there was some obstacle connected with her father, which forbade her to listen to my offer of marriage. From the time when she had accidentally looked toward the red-brick house, something in her manner that it is quite impossible to describe had suggested to my mind that this obstacle was not only something she could not mention, but something that she was partly ashamed of, partly afraid of, and partly doubtful about. What could it be? How had she first known it? In what way was her father connected with it?

In the course of our walks she had told me nothing about herself that was not perfectly simple and unsuggestive.

Her childhood had been passed in England. After that, she had lived with her father and mother at Paris, where the doctor had many friends – for all of whom she remembered feeling more or less dislike, without being able to tell why. They had then come to England, and had lived in lodgings in London. For a time they had been miserably poor. But, after her mother's death – a sudden death from heart disease – there had come a change in their affairs, which she was quite unable to explain. They had removed to their present abode, to give the doctor full accommodation for the carrying on of his scientific pursuits. He often had occasion to go to London, but never took her with him. The only woman at home now, beside herself, was an elderly person, who acted as cook and housekeeper, and who had been in their service for many years. It was very lonely sometimes not having a companion of her own age and sex, but she had got tolerably used to bear it, and to amuse herself with her books, and music, and flowers.

Thus far she chatted about herself quite freely, but when I tried, even in the vaguest manner, to lead her into discussing the causes of her strangely secluded life, she looked so distressed, and became so suddenly silent, that I naturally refrained from saying another word on that topic. One conclusion, however, I felt tolerably sure that I had drawn correctly from what she said: her father's conduct toward her, though not absolutely blameable or grossly neglectful on any point, had still never been of a nature to make her ardently fond of him. He performed the ordinary parental duties rigidly and respectably enough, but he had apparently not cared to win all the filial love that his daughter would have bestowed on a more affectionate man.

When, after reflecting on what Alicia had told me, I began to call to mind what I had been able to observe for myself, I found ample materials to excite my curiosity in relation to the doctor, if not my distrust.

I have already described how I heard the clang of the heavy door on the occasion of my first visit to the red-brick house. The next day, when the doctor again took leave of me in the hall, I hit on a plan for seeing the door as well as hearing it. I dawdled on my way out, till I heard the clang again; then pretended to remember some important message that I had forgotten to give to the doctor, and with a look of innocent hurry ran upstairs to overtake him. The disguised workman ran after me with a shout of 'Stop!' I was conveniently deaf to him – reached the first floor landing – and arrived at a door that shut off the whole staircase higher up, an iron door, as solid as if it belonged to a banker's strongroom, and guarded millions of money. I returned to the hall, inattentive to the servant's not over-civil remonstrances, and, saying that I would wait till I saw the doctor again, left the house.

The next day two pale-looking men, in artisan costume, came up to the gate at the same time as I did, each carrying a long wooden box under his arm, strongly bound with iron. I tried to make them talk while we were waiting for admission, but neither of them would go beyond 'Yes,' or 'No', and both had, to my eyes, some unmistakably sinister lines in their faces. The next day the housekeeping cook came to the door – a buxom old woman with a look and a ready smile, and something in her manner that suggested that she had not begun life quite so respectably as she was now ending it. She seemed to be decidedly satisfied with my personal appearance; talked to me on indifferent matters with great glibness; but suddenly became silent and diplomatic the moment I looked toward the stair and asked innocently if she had to go up and down them often in the course of the day. As for the doctor himself, he was unapproachable on the subject of the mysterious upper regions. If I introduced chemistry in general into the conversation he begged me not to spoil his happy holiday hours with his daughter and me by leading him back to his workaday thoughts. If I referred to his own experiments in particular he always made a joke about being afraid of my chemical knowledge, and of my wishing to anticipate him in his discoveries. In brief, after a week's run of the lower regions, the upper part of the red-brick house and the actual nature of its owner's occupations still remained impenetrable mysteries to me, pry, ponder, and question as I might.

Thinking of this on the riverbank, in connection with the distressing scene that I had just had with Alicia, I found that the mysterious obstacle at which she had hinted, the mysterious life led by her father, and the mysterious top of the house that had hitherto defied my curiosity, all three connected themselves in my mind as links of the same chain. The obstacle to my marrying Alicia was the thing that most troubled me. If I only found out what it was, and if I made light of it (which I was resolved beforehand to do, let it be what it might), I should most probably end by overcoming her scruples, and taking her away from the ominous red-brick house in the character of my wife. But how was I to make the all-important discovery?

Cudgelling my brains for an answer to this question, I fell at last into reasoning upon it, by a process of natural logic, something after this fashion: The mysterious top of the house is connected with the doctor, and the doctor is connected with the obstacle that has made wretchedness between Alicia and me. If I can only get to the top of the house, I may get also to the root of the obstacle. It is a dangerous and an uncertain experiment; but, come what may of it, I will try and find out, if human ingenuity can compass the means, what Dr Dulcifer's occupation really is, on the other side of that iron door.

Having come to this resolution (and deriving, let me add, parenthetically, great consolation from it), the next subject of consideration was the best method of getting safely into the top regions of the house.

Picking the lock of the iron door was out of the question, from the exposed nature of the situation that that mysterious iron barrier occupied. My only possible way to the second floor lay by the back of the house. I had looked up at it two or three times, while walking in the garden after dinner with Alicia. What had I brought away in my memory as the result of that casual inspection of my host's back premises? Several fragments of useful information.

In the first place, one of the most magnificent vines I had ever seen grew against the back wall of the house, trained carefully on a strong trellis-work. In the second place, the middle first-floor back window looked out on a little stone balcony, built on the top of the porch over the garden door. In the third place, the back windows of the second floor had been open on each occasion when I had seen them – most probably to air the house, which could not be ventilated from the front during the hot summer weather, in consequence of the shut-up condition of all the windows thereabouts. In the fourth place, hard by the coach house in which Dr Dulcifer's neat gig was put up, there was a tool-shed, in which the gardener kept his short pruning-ladder. In the fifth and last place, outside the stable in which Dr Dulcifer's blood mare lived in luxurious solitude, was a dog-kennel with a large mastiff chained to it night and day. If I could only rid myself of the dog – a gaunt, half-starved brute, made savage and mangy by perpetual confinement – I did not see any reason to despair of getting in undiscovered at one of the second-floor windows – provided I waited until a sufficiently late hour, and succeeded in scaling the garden wall at the back of the house.

Life without Alicia being not worth having, I determined to risk the thing that very night.

Going back at once to the town of Barkingham, I provided myself with a short bit of rope, a little bullseye lantern, a small screwdriver, and a nice bit of beef chemically adapted for the soothing of troublesome dogs. I then dressed, disposed of these things neatly in my coat pockets, and went to the doctor's to dinner. In one respect, fortune favoured my audacity. It was the sultriest day of the whole season – surely they could not think of shutting up the second-floor back windows tonight!

Alicia was pale and silent. The lovely brown eyes, when they looked at me, said as plainly as in words, 'We have been crying a great deal, Frank, since we saw you last.' The little white fingers gave mine a significant squeeze – and that was all the reference that passed between us to what happened in the morning. She sat through the dinner bravely, but, when the dessert came, left us for the night, with a few shy, hurried words about the excessive heat of the weather being too much for her. I rose to open the door, and exchanged a last meaning look with her, as she bowed and went by me. Little did I think that I should have to live upon nothing but the remembrance of that look for many weary days that were yet to come.

The doctor was in excellent spirits, and almost oppressively hospitable. We sat sociably chatting over our claret till past eight o'clock. Then my host turned to his desk to write a letter before the post want out, and I strolled away to smoke a cigar in the garden.

Second-floor back windows all open, atmosphere as sultry as ever, gardener's pruning-ladder quite safe in the tool-shed, savage mastiff in his kennel crunching his bones for supper. Good. The dog will not be visited again tonight: I may throw my medicated bit of beef at once into his kennel. I acted on the idea immediately; the dog seized his piece of beef; I heard a snap, a wheeze, a choke, and a groan – and there was the mastiff disposed of, inside the kennel, where nobody could find out that he was dead till the time came for feeding him the next morning.

I went back to the doctor; we had a social glass of cold brandy and water together; I lighted another cigar, and took my leave. My host being too respectable a man not to keep early country hours, I went away, as usual, about ten. The mysterious manservant locked the gate behind me. I sauntered on the road back to Barkingham for about five minutes, then struck off sharp for the plantation, lighted my lantern with the help of my cigar and a brimstone match of that barbarous period, shut down the slide again, and made for the garden wall.

It was formidably high, and garnished horribly with broken bottles; but it was also old, and when I came to pick at the mortar with my screwdriver, I found it reasonably rotten with age and damp.

I removed four bricks to make foot holes in different positions up the wall. It was desperately hard and long work, easy as it may sound in description – especially when I had to hold on by the top of the wall, with my flat opera hat (as we used to call it in those days) laid, as a guard, between my hand and the glass, while I cleared a way through the sharp bottle-ends for my other hand and my knees. This done, my great difficulty was vanquished, and I had only to drop luxuriously into a flower bed on the other side of the wall.

Perfect stillness in the garden, no sign of a light anywhere at the back of the house, first-floor windows all shut, second-floor windows still open. I fetched the pruning-ladder, put it against the side of the porch, tied one end of my bit of rope to the top round of it, took the other end in my mouth, and prepared to climb to the balcony over the porch by the thick vine branches and the trellis-work.

No man who has had any real experience of life can have failed to observe how amazingly close, in critical situations, the grotesque and the terrible, the comic and the serious, contrive to tread on each other's heels. At such times, the last thing we ought properly to think of comes into our heads, or the least consistent event that could possibly be expected to happen does actually occur. When I put my life in danger on that memorable night by putting my foot on the trellis-work, I absolutely thought of the never-dying Lady Malkinshaw plunged in refreshing slumber, and of the frantic exclamations Mr Batterbury would utter if he saw what her ladyship's grandson was doing with his precious life and limbs at that critical moment. I am no hero – I was fully aware of the danger to which I was exposing myself; and yet I protest that I caught myself laughing under my breath, with the most outrageous inconsistency, at the instant when I began the ascent of the trellis-work.

I reached the balcony over the porch in safety, depending more upon the tough vine branches than the trellis-work during my ascent. My next employment was to pull up the pruning-ladder, as softly as possible, by the rope that I held attached to it. This done, I put the ladder against the house wall, listened, measured the distance to the open second-floor window with my eye, listened again – and, finding all quiet, began my second and last ascent. The ladder was comfortably long, and I was conveniently tall; my hand was on the window sill – I mounted another two rounds – and my eyes were level with the interior of the room.

Suppose any one should be sleeping there!

I listened at the window attentively before I ventured on taking my lantern out of my coat pocket. The night was so quiet and airless that there was not the faintest rustle among the leaves in the garden beneath me to distract my attention. I listened. The breathing of the lightest of sleepers must have reached my ear, through that intense stillness, if the room had been a bedroom, and the bed were occupied. I heard nothing but the quick beat of my own heart. The minutes of suspense were passing heavily – I laid my other hand over the window-sill, then a moment of doubt came – doubt whether I should carry the adventure any further. I mastered my hesitation directly – it was too late for second thoughts. 'Now for it!' I whispered to myself, and got in at the window.

To wait, listening again, in the darkness of that unknown region, was more than I had courage for. The moment I was down on the floor, I pulled the lantern out of my pocket and raised the shade.

So far, so good – I found myself in a dirty lumber room. Large pans, some of them cracked and more of them broken; empty boxes bound with iron, of the same sort as those I had seen the workmen bringing in at the front gate; old coal sacks; a packing case full of coke; and a huge, cracked, mouldy blacksmith's bellows – these were the principal objects that I observed in the lumber room. The one door leading out of it was open, as I had expected it would be, in order to let the air through the back window into the house. I took off my shoes, and stole into the passage. My first impulse, the moment I looked along it, was to shut down my lantern-shade, and listen again.

Still I heard nothing, but at the far end of the passage I saw a bright light pouring through the half-opened door of one of the mysterious front rooms.

I crept softly toward it. A decidedly chemical smell began to steal into my nostrils – and, listening again, I thought I heard above me, and in some distant room, a noise like the low growl of a large furnace, muffled in some peculiar manner. Should I retrace my steps in that direction? No – not till I had seen something of the room with the bright light, outside of which I was now standing. I bent forward softly, looking by little and little further and further through the opening of the door, until my head and shoulders were fairly inside the room, and my eyes had convinced me that no living soul, sleeping or waking, was in any part of it at that particular moment. Impelled by a fatal curiosity, I entered immediately, and began to look about me with eager eyes.

I saw iron ladles, pans full of white sand, files with white metal left glittering in their teeth, moulds of plaster of Paris, bags containing the same material in powder, a powerful machine with the name and use of which I was theoretically not unacquainted, white metal in a partially fused state, bottles of aquafortis, dies scattered over a dresser, crucibles, sand-paper, bars of metal, and edged tools in plenty, of the strangest construction. I was not at all a scrupulous man, as the reader knows by this time; but when I looked at these objects, and thought of Alicia, I could not for the life of me help shuddering. There was not the least doubt about it, even after the little I had seen: the important chemical pursuits to which Dr Dulcifer was devoting himself, meant, in plain English and in one word – coining.

Did Alicia know what I knew now, or did she only suspect it?

Whichever way I answered that question in my own mind, I could be no longer at any loss for an explanation of her behaviour in the meadow by the stream, or of that unnaturally gloomy, downcast look that overspread her face when her father's pursuits were the subject of conversation. Did I falter in my resolution to marry her, now that I had discovered what the obstacle was that had made mystery and wretchedness between us? Certainly not. I was above all prejudices. I was the least particular of mankind. I had no family affection in my way – and, greatest fact of all, I was in love. Under those circumstances what Rogue of any spirit would have faltered? After the first shock of the discovery was over, my resolution to be Alicia's husband was settled more firmly than ever.

There was a little round table in a corner of the room furthest from the door, which I had not yet examined. A feverish longing to look at everything within my reach – to penetrate to the innermost recesses of the labyrinth in which I had involved myself – consumed me. I went to the table and saw upon it, ranged symmetrically side by side, four objects that looked like thick rulers wrapped up in silver paper. I opened the paper at the end of one of the rulers, and found that it was composed of half-crowns. I had closed the paper again, and was just raising my head from the table over which it had been bent, when my right cheek came in contact with something hard and cold. I started back – looked up – and confronted Dr Dulcifer, holding a pistol at my right temple.

IX

The doctor (like me) had his shoes off. The doctor (like me) had come in without making the least noise. He cocked the pistol without saying a word. I felt that I was probably standing face to face with death, and I too said not a word. We two Rogues looked each other steadily and silently in the face – he, the mighty and prosperous villain, with my life in his hands; I, the abject and poor scamp, waiting his mercy.

It must have been at least a minute after I heard the click of the cocked pistol before he spoke.

'How did you get here?' he asked.

The quiet commonplace terms in which he put his question, and the perfect composure and politeness of his manner, reminded me a little of Gentleman Jones. But the doctor was much the more respectable-looking man of the two: his baldness was more intellectual and benevolent; there was a delicacy and propriety in the pulpiness of his fat white chin, a bland bagginess in his unwhiskered cheeks, a reverent roughness about his eyebrows and a fullness in his lower eyelids, which raised him far higher, physiognomically speaking, in the social scale, than my old prison acquaintance. Put a shovel-hat on Gentleman Jones and the effect would only have been eccentric; put the same covering on the head of Dr Dulcifer and the effect would have been strictly episcopal.

'How did you get here?' he repeated, still without showing the least irritation.

I told him how I had got in at the second-floor window, without concealing a word of the truth. The gravity of the situation, and the sharpness of the doctor's intellects, as expressed in his eyes, made anything like a suppression of facts on my part a desperately dangerous experiment.

'You wanted to see what I was about up here, did you?' said he, when I had ended my confession. 'Do you know?'

The pistol barrel touched my cheek as he said the last words. I thought of all the suspicious objects scattered about the room, of the probability that he was only putting this question to try my courage, of the very likely chance that he would shoot me forthwith if I began to prevaricate. I thought of these things and boldly answered:

'Yes, I do know.'

He looked at me reflectively, then said, in low, thoughtful tones, speaking, not to me, but entirely to himself:

'Suppose I shoot him?'

I saw in his eye that if I flinched, he would draw the trigger.

'Suppose you trust me?' I said, without moving a muscle.

'I trusted you, as an honest man, downstairs, and I find you, like a thief, up here,' returned the doctor, with a self-satisfied smile at the neatness of his own retort. 'No,' he continued, relapsing into soliloquy, 'there is risk every way; but the least risk perhaps is to shoot him.'

'Wrong,' said I. 'There are relations of mine who have a pecuniary interest in my life. I am the main condition of a contingent reversion in their favour. If I am missed, I shall be enquired after.' I have wondered since at my own coolness in the face of the doctor's pistol, but my life depended on my keeping my self-possession, and the desperate nature of the situation lent me a desperate courage.

'How do I know you are not lying?' he asked.

'Have I not spoken the truth, hitherto?'

Those words made him hesitate. He lowered the pistol slowly to his side. I began to breathe freely.

'Trust me,' I repeated. 'If you don't believe I would hold my tongue about what I have seen here, for your sake, you may be certain that I would for – '

'For my daughter's,' he interposed, with a sarcastic smile.

I bowed with all imaginable cordiality. The doctor waved his pistol in the air contemptuously.

'There are two ways of making you hold your tongue,' he said. 'The first is shooting you; the second is making a felon of you. On consideration, after what you have said, the risk in either case seems about equal. I am naturally a humane man; your family have done me no injury; I will not be the cause of their losing money; I won't take your life, I'll have your character. We are all felons on this floor of the house. You have come among us – you shall be one of us. Ring that bell.'

He pointed with the pistol to a bell-handle behind me. I pulled it in silence.

Felon! The word has an ugly sound – a very ugly sound. But, considering how near the black curtain had been to falling over the adventurous drama of my life, had I any right to complain of the prolongation of the scene, however darkly it might look at first? Besides, some of the best feelings of our common nature (putting out of all question the value that men so unaccountably persist in setting on their own lives) impelled me, of necessity, to choose the alternative of felonious existence in preference to that of respectable death. Love and honour bade me live to marry Alicia, and a sense of family duty made me shrink from occasioning a loss of three thousand pounds to my affectionate sister. Perish the far-fetched scruples that would break the heart of one lovely woman, and scatter to the winds the pin money of another!

'If you utter one word in contradiction of anything I say when my workmen come into the room,' said the doctor, uncocking his pistol as soon as I had rung the bell, 'I shall change my mind about leaving your life and taking your character. Remember that, and keep a guard on your tongue.'

The door opened, and four men entered. One was an old man whom I had not seen before; in the other three I recognised the workman-like footman, and the two sinister artisans whom I had met at the house-gate. They all started, guiltily enough, at seeing me.

'Let me introduce you,' said the doctor, taking me by the arm. 'Old File and Young File, Mill and Screw – Mr Frank Softly. We have nicknames in this workshop, Mr Softly, derived humorously from our professional tools and machinery. When you have been here long enough, you will get a nickname, too. Gentlemen,' he continued, turning to the workmen, 'this is a new recruit, with a knowledge of chemistry that will be useful to us. He is perfectly well aware that the nature of our vocation makes us suspicious of all newcomers, and he, therefore, desires to give you practical proof that he is to be depended on, by making half-a-crown immediately, and sending the same up, along with our handiwork, directed in his own handwriting, to our estimable correspondents in London. When you have all seen him do this of his own free will, and thereby put his own life as completely within the power of the law as we have put ours, you will know that he is really one of us, and will be under no apprehensions for the future. Take great pains with him, and as soon as he turns out a tolerably neat article, from the simple flatted plates, under your inspection, let me know. I shall take a few hours' repose on my camp bed in the study, and shall be found there whenever you want me.'

He nodded to us all round in the most friendly manner, and left the room.

I looked with considerable secret distrust at the four gentlemen who were to instruct me in the art of making false coin. Young File was the workman-like footman; Old File was his father; Mill and Screw were the two sinister artisans. The man of the company whose looks I liked least was Screw. He had wicked little twinkling eyes – and they followed me about treacherously whenever I moved. 'You and I, Screw, are likely to quarrel,' I thought to myself, as I tried vainly to stare him out of countenance.

I entered on my new and felonious functions forthwith. Resistance was useless, and calling for help would have been sheer insanity. It was midnight; and, even supposing the windows had not been barred, the house was a mile from any human habitation. Accordingly, I abandoned myself to fate with my usual magnanimity. Only let me end in winning Alicia and I am resigned to the loss of whatever small shreds and patches of respectability still hang about me – such was my philosophy. I wish I could have taken higher moral ground with equally consoling results to my own feelings.

The same regard for the well-being of society that led me to abstain from entering into particulars on the subject of old master-making, when I was apprenticed to Mr Ishmael Pickup, now commands me to be equally discreet on the kindred subject of half-crown-making, under the auspices of Old File, Young File, Mill, and Screw.

Let me merely record that I was a kind of machine in the hands of these four skilled workmen. I moved from room to room, and from process to process, the creature of their directing eyes and guiding hands. I cut myself, I burned myself, I got speechless from fatigue, and giddy from want of sleep. In short, the sun of the new day was high in the heavens before it was necessary to disturb Dr Dulcifer. It had absolutely taken me almost as long to manufacture a half-a-crown feloniously as it takes a respectable man to make it honestly. This is saying a great deal, but it is literally true for all that.

Looking quite fresh and rosy after his night's sleep, the doctor inspected my coin with the air of a schoolmaster examining a little boy's exercise, then handed it to Old File to put the finished touches and correct the mistakes. It was afterward returned to me. My own hand placed it in one of the rouleaux of false half-crowns; and my own hand also directed the spurious coin, when it had been safely packed up, to a certain London dealer who was to be on the lookout for it by the next night's mail. That done, my initiation was so far complete.

'I have sent for your luggage, and paid your bill at the inn,' said the doctor; 'of course in your name. You are now to enjoy the hospitality that I could not extend to you before. A room upstairs has been prepared for you. You are not exactly in a state of confinement, but, until your studies are completed, I think you had better not interrupt them by going out.'

'A prisoner!' I exclaimed aghast.

'Prisoner is a hard word,' answered the doctor. 'Let us say, a guest under surveillance.'

'Do you seriously mean that you intend to keep me shut up in this part of the house, at your will and pleasure?' I enquired, my heart sinking lower and lower at every word I spoke.

'It is very spacious and airy,' said the doctor; 'as for the lower part of the house, you would find no company there, so you can't want to go to it.'

'No company!' I repeated faintly.

'No. My daughter went away this morning for change of air and scene, accompanied by my housekeeper. You look astonished, my dear sir – let me frankly explain myself. While you were the respectable son of Dr Softly, and grandson of

88

Lady Malkinshaw, I was ready enough to let my daughter associate with you, and should not have objected if you had married her off my hands into a highly connected family. Now, however, when you are nothing but one of the workmen in my manufactory of money, your social position is seriously altered for the worse; and, as I could not possibly think of you for a son-in-law, I have considered it best to prevent all chance of your communicating with Alicia again, by sending her away from this house while you are in it. You will be in it until I have completed certain business arrangements now in a forward state of progress – after that, you may go away if you please. Pray remember that you have to thank yourself for the position you now stand in, and do me the justice to admit that my conduct toward you is remarkably straightforward, and perfectly natural under all the circumstances.'

These words fairly overwhelmed me. I did not even make an attempt to answer them. The hard trials to my courage, endurance, and physical strength, through which I had passed within the last twelve hours, had completely exhausted all my powers of resistance. I went away speechless to my own room, and when I found myself alone there, burst out crying. Childish, was it not?

When I had been rested and strengthened by a few hours' sleep, I found myself able to confront the future with tolerable calmness.

What would it be best for me to do? Ought I to attempt to make my escape? I did not despair of succeeding, but when I began to think of the consequences of success, I hesitated. My chief object now was, not so much to secure my own freedom, as to find my way to Alicia. I had never been so deeply and desperately in love with her as I was now, when I knew she was separated from me. Suppose I succeeded in escaping from the clutches of Dr Dulcifer – might I not be casting myself use-lessly on the world, without a chance of finding a single clue to trace her by? Suppose, on the other hand, that I remained for the present in the red-brick house – should I not by that course of conduct be putting myself in the best position for making discoveries?

In the first place, there was the chance that Alicia might find some secret means of communicating with me if I remained where I was. In the second place, the doctor would, in all probability, have occasion to write to his daughter, or would be likely to receive letters from her; and, if I quieted all suspicion on my account, by docile behaviour, and kept my eyes sharply on the lookout, I might find opportunities of surprising the secrets of his writing-desk. I felt that I need be under no restraints of honour with a man who was keeping me a prisoner, and who had made an accomplice of me by threatening my life. Accordingly, while resolving to show outwardly an amiable submission to my fate, I determined at the same time to keep secretly on the watch, and to take the very first chance of outwitting Dr Dulcifer that might happen to present itself. When we next met I was perfectly civil to him. He was too well-bred a man not to match me on the common ground of courtesy.

'Permit me to congratulate you,' he said, 'on the improve-ment in your manner and appearance. You are beginning well, Francis. Go on as you have begun.'

X

My first few days' experience in my new position satisfied me that Dr Dulcifer preserved himself from betrayal by a system of surveillance worthy of the very worst days of the Holy Inquisition itself.

No man of us ever knew that he was not being overlooked at home, or followed when he went out, by another man. Peepholes were pierced in the wall of each room, and we were never certain, while at work, whose eye was observing, or whose ear was listening in secret. Though we all lived together, we were probably the least united body of men ever assembled under one roof. By way of effectually keeping up the want of union between us, we were not all trusted alike. I soon discovered that Old File and Young File were much further advanced in the doctor's confidence than Mill, Screw, or myself. There was a locked-up room, and a continually closed door shutting off a back staircase, of both of which Old File and Young File possessed keys that were never so much as trusted in the possession of the rest of us. There was also a trapdoor in the floor of the principal workroom, the use of which was known to nobody but the doctor and his two privileged men. If we had not been all nearly on an equality in the matter of wages, these distinctions would have made bad blood among us. As it was, nobody having reason to complain of unjustly diminished wages, nobody cared about any preferences in which profit was not involved.

The doctor must have gained a great deal of money by his skill as a coiner. His profits in business could never have averaged less than five hundred per cent; and, to do him justice, he was really a generous as well as a rich master.

Even I, as a new hand, was, in fair proportion, as well paid by the week as the rest.

We, of course, had nothing to do with the passing of false money – we only manufactured it (sometimes at the rate of four hundred pounds' worth in a week), and left its circulation to be managed by our customers in London and the large towns. Whatever we paid for in Barkingham was paid for in the genuine mint coinage. I used often to compare my own true guineas, half-crowns and shillings with our imitations under the doctor's supervision, and was always amazed at the resemblance. Our scientific chief had discovered a process something like what is called electrotyping nowadays, as I imagine. He was very proud of this, but he was prouder still of the ring of his metal, and with reason: it must have been a nice ear indeed that could discover the false tones in the doctor's coinage.

If I had been the most scrupulous man in the world, I must still have received my wages, for the very necessary purpose of not appearing to distinguish myself invidiously from my fellow-workmen. Upon the whole, I got on well with them. Old File and I struck up quite a friendship. Young File and Mill worked harmoniously with me, but Screw and I (as I had foreboded) quarrelled.

This last man was not on good terms with his fellows, and had less of the doctor's confidence than any of the rest of us. Naturally not of a sweet temper, his isolated position in the house had soured him, and he rashly attempted to vent his ill humour on me, as a newcomer. For some days I bore with him patiently; but at last he got the better of my powers of endurance, and I gave him a lesson in manners, one day, on the educational system of Gentleman Jones. He did not return the blow, or complain to the doctor; he only looked at me wickedly,

and said: 'I'll be even with you for that, some of these days.'
I soon forgot the words and the look.

With Old File, as I have said, I became quite friendly.
Excepting the secrets of our prison-house, he was ready
enough to talk on subjects about which I was curious.

He had known his present master as a young man, and was
perfectly familiar with all the events of his career. From various
conversations, at odds and ends of spare time, I discovered
that Dr Dulcifer had begun life as a footman in a gentleman's
family; that his young mistress had eloped with him, taking
away with her every article of value that was her own personal
property, in the shape of jewellery and dresses; that they had
lived upon the sale of these things for some time; and that the
husband, when the wife's means were exhausted, had turned
strolling-player for a year or two. Abandoning that pursuit,
he had next become a quack-doctor, first in a resident, then
in a vagabond capacity – taking a medical degree of his own
conferring, and holding to it as a good travelling title for the
rest of his life. From the selling of quack medicines he had
proceeded to the adulterating of foreign wines, varied by
lucrative evening occupation in the Paris gambling houses.
On returning to his native land, he still continued to turn
his chemical knowledge to account, by giving his services to
that particular branch of our commercial industry that is
commonly described as the adulteration of commodities; and
from this he had gradually risen to the more refined pursuit of
adulterating gold and silver – or, to use the common phrase
again, making bad money.

According to Old File's statement, though Dr Dulcifer had
never actually ill-used his wife, he had never lived on kind
terms with her: the main cause of the estrangement between
them, in later years, being Mrs Dulcifer's resolute resistance to

her husband's plans for emerging from poverty by the simple process of coining his own money. The poor woman still held fast by some of the principles imparted to her in happier days, and she was devotedly fond of her daughter. At the time of her sudden death, she was secretly making arrangements to leave the doctor, and find a refuge for herself and her child in a foreign country, under the care of the one friend of her family who had not cast her off. Questioning my informant about Alicia next, I found that he knew very little about her relations with her father in later years. That she must long since have discovered him to be not quite so respectable a man as he looked, and that she might suspect something wrong was going on in the house at the present time, were, in Old File's opinion, matters of certainty; but that she knew anything positively on the subject of her father's occupations, he seemed to doubt. The doctor was not the sort of man to give his daughter, or any other woman, the slightest chance of surprising his secrets.

These particulars I gleaned during one long month of servitude and imprisonment in the fatal red-brick house.

During all that time not the slightest intimation reached me of Alicia's whereabouts. Had she forgotten me? I could not believe it. Unless the dear brown eyes were the falsest hypocrites in the world, it was impossible that she should have forgotten me. Was she watched? Were all means of communicating with me, even in secret, carefully removed from her? I looked oftener and oftener into the doctor's study as those questions occurred to me, but he never quitted it without locking the writing-desk first – he never left any papers scattered on the table, and he was never absent from the room at any special times and seasons that could be previously calculated upon. I began to despair, and to feel in my lonely moments a yearning to renew that childish experiment of crying, which I have already adverted to, in the way of confession. Moralists will be glad to hear that I really suffered acute mental misery at this time of my life. My state of depression would have gratified the most exacting of Methodists, and my penitent face would have made my fortune if I could only have been exhibited by a reformatory association on the platform of Exeter Hall.

How much longer was this to last? Whither should I turn my steps when I regained my freedom? In what direction throughout all England should I begin to look for Alicia?

Sleeping and walking – working and idling – those were now my constant thoughts. I did my best to prepare myself for every emergency that could happen; I tried to arm myself beforehand against every possible accident that could befall me. While I was still hard at work sharpening my faculties and disciplining my energies in this way, an accident befell the doctor, on the possibility of which I had not dared to calculate, even in my most hopeful moments.

XI

One morning I was engaged in the principal workroom with my employer. We were alone. Old File and his son were occupied in the garrets. Screw had been sent to Barkingham, accompanied, on the usual precautionary plan, by Mill. They had been gone nearly an hour when the doctor sent me into the next room to moisten and knead up some plaster of Paris. While I was engaged in this occupation, I suddenly heard strange voices in the large workroom. My curiosity was instantly excited. I drew back the little shutter from the peephole in the wall, and looked through it.

I saw first my old enemy, Screw, with his villainous face much paler than usual; next, two respectably dressed strangers whom he appeared to have brought into the room; and next to them Young File, addressing himself to the doctor.

'I beg your pardon, sir,' said my friend, the workman-like footman, 'but before these gentlemen say anything for themselves, I wish to explain, as they seem strangers to you, that I only let them in after I had heard them give the password. My instructions are to let anybody in on our side of the door if they can give the password. No offence, sir, but I want it to be understood that I have done my duty.'

'Quite right, my man,' said the doctor, in his blandest manner. 'You may go back to your work.'

Young File left the room, with a scrutinising look for the two strangers and a suspicious frown for Screw.

'Allow us to introduce ourselves,' began the elder of the two strangers.

'Pardon me for a moment,' interposed the doctor. 'Where is Mill?' he added, turning to Screw.

'Doing our errands at Barkingham,' answered Screw, turning paler than ever.

'We happened to meet your two men, and to ask them the way to your house,' said the stranger who had just spoken. 'This man, with a caution that does him infinite credit, required to know our business before he told us. We managed to introduce the password – "Happy-go-lucky" – into our answer. This of course quieted suspicion, and he, at our request, guided us here, leaving his fellow-workman, as he has just told you, to do all errands at Barkingham.'

While these words were being spoken, I saw Screw's eyes wandering discontentedly and amazedly round the room. He had left me in it with the doctor before he went out: was he disappointed at not finding me in it on his return?

While this thought was passing through my mind, the stranger resumed his explanations.

'We are here,' he said, 'as agents appointed to transact private business, out of London, for Mr Manasseh, with whom you have dealings, I think?'

'Certainly,' said the doctor, with a smile.

'And who owes you a little account, which we are appointed to settle.'

'Just so!' remarked the doctor, pleasantly rubbing his hands one over the other. 'My good friend, Mr Manasseh, does not like to trust the post, I suppose? Very glad to make your acquaintance, gentlemen. Have you got the little memorandum about you?'

'Yes, but we think there is a slight inaccuracy in it. Have you any objection to let us refer to your ledger?'

'Not the least in the world. Screw, go down into my private laboratory, open the table-drawer nearest the window, and bring up a locked book, with a parchment cover, which you will find in it.'

As Screw obeyed I saw a look pass between him and the two strangers that made me begin to feel a little uneasy. I thought the doctor noticed it too, but he preserved his countenance, as usual, in a state of the most unruffled composure.

'What a time that fellow is gone!' he exclaimed gaily. 'Perhaps I had better go and get the book myself.'

The two strangers had been gradually lessening the distance between the doctor and themselves, ever since Screw had left the room. The last words were barely out of his mouth, before they both sprang upon him, and pinioned his arms with their hands.

'Steady, my fine fellow,' said Mr Manasseh's head agent. 'It's no go. We are Bow Street runners, and we've got you for coining.'

'Not a doubt of it,' said the doctor, with the most superb coolness. 'You needn't hold me. I'm not fool enough to resist when I'm fairly caught.'

'Wait till we've searched you, and then we'll talk about that,' said the runner.*

The doctor submitted to the searching with the patience of a martyr. No offensive weapon being found in his pockets, they allowed him to sit down unmolested in the nearest chair.

'Screw, I suppose?' said the doctor, looking enquiringly at the officers.

'Exactly,' said the principal man of the two. 'We have been secretly corresponding with him for weeks past. We have nabbed the man who went out with him, and got him safe at Barkingham. Don't expect Screw back with the ledger. As soon

* The 'Bow Street runners' of those days were the predecessors of the detective police of the present time.

as he has made sure that the rest of you are in the house, he is to fetch another man or two of our Bow Street lot, who are waiting outside till they hear from us. We only want an old man and a young one, and a third pal of yours who is a gentleman born, to make a regular clearance in the house. When we have once got you all, it will be the prettiest capture that's ever been made since I was in the force.'

What the doctor answered to this I cannot say. Just as the officer had done speaking, I heard footsteps approaching the room in which I was listening. Was Screw looking for me? I instantly closed the peephole and got behind the door. It opened back upon me, and, sure enough, Screw entered cautiously.

An empty old wardrobe stood opposite the door. Evidently suspecting that I might have taken the alarm and concealed myself inside it, he approached it on tiptoe. On tiptoe also I followed him, and, just as his hands were on the wardrobe door, my hands were on his throat. He was a little man, and no match for me. I easily and gently laid him on his back, in a voiceless and half-suffocated state – throwing myself right over him, to keep his legs quiet. When I saw his face getting black, and his small eyes growing largely globular, I let go with one hand, crammed my empty plaster of Paris bag, which lay close by, into his mouth, tied it fast, secured his hands and feet, and then left him perfectly harmless, while I took counsel with myself how best to secure my own safety.

I should have made my escape at once, but for what I heard the officer say about the men who were waiting outside. Were they waiting near or at a distance? Were they on the watch at the front or the back of the house? I thought it highly desirable to give myself a chance of ascertaining their whereabouts from the talk of the officers in the next room, before I risked the possibility of running right into their clutches on the outer side of the door.

I cautiously opened the peephole once more.

The doctor appeared to be still on the most friendly terms with his vigilant guardians from Bow Street.

'Have you any objection to my ringing for some lunch, before we are all taken off to London together?' I heard him ask in his most cheerful tones. 'A glass of wine and a bit of bread and cheese won't do you any harm, gentlemen, if you are as hungry as I am.'

'If you want to eat and drink, order the victuals at once,' replied one of the runners, sulkily. 'We don't happen to want anything ourselves.'

'Sorry for it,' said the doctor. 'I have some of the best old Madeira in England.'

'Like enough,' retorted the officer sarcastically. 'But you see we are not quite such fools as we look, and we have heard of such a thing, in our time, as hocussed wine.'

'O fie! fie!' exclaimed the doctor merrily. 'Remember how well I am behaving myself, and don't wound my feelings by suspecting me of such shocking treachery as that!'

He moved to a corner of the room behind him, and touched a knob in the wall that I had never before observed. A bell rang directly, which had a new tone in it to my ears.

'Too bad,' said the doctor, turning round again to the runners, 'really too bad, gentlemen, to suspect me of that!'

Shaking his head deprecatingly, he moved back to the corner, pulled aside something in the wall, disclosed the mouth of a pipe that was a perfect novelty to me, and called down it.

'Moses!'

It was the first time I had heard that name in the house.

'Who is Moses?' enquired the officers both together, advancing on him suspiciously.

'Only my servant,' answered the doctor. He turned once more to the pipe, and called down it: 'Bring up the Stilton cheese, and a bottle of the old Madeira.'

The cheese we had in use at that time was of purely Dutch extraction. I remembered port, sherry, and claret in my palmy dinner-days at the doctor's family table, but certainly not old Madeira. Perhaps he selfishly kept his best wine and his choicest cheese for his own consumption.

'Sam,' said one of the runners to the other, 'you look to our civil friend here, and I'll grab Moses when he brings up the lunch.'

'Would you like to see what the operation of coining is, while my man is getting the lunch ready?' said the doctor. 'It may be of use to me at the trial, if you can testify that I afforded you every facility for finding out anything you might want to know. Only mention my polite anxiety to make things easy and instructive from the very first, and I may get recommended to mercy. See here – this queer-looking machine, gentlemen (from which two of my men derive their nicknames), is what we call a mill-and-screw.'

He began to explain the machine with the manner and tone of a lecturer at a scientific institution. In spite of themselves, the officers burst out laughing. I looked round at Screw as the doctor got deeper into his explanations. The traitor was rolling his wicked eyes horribly at me. They presented so shocking a sight that I looked away again. What was I to do next? The minutes were getting on, and I had not heard a word yet, through the peephole, on the subject of the reserve of Bow Street runners outside. Would it not be best to risk everything, and get away at once by the back of the house?

Just as I had resolved on venturing the worst, and making my escape forthwith, I heard the officers interrupt the doctor's lecture.

'Your lunch is a long time coming,' said one of them.

'Moses is lazy,' answered the doctor, 'and the Madeira is in a remote part of the cellar. Shall I ring again?'

'Hang your ringing again!' growled the runner, impatiently. 'I don't understand why our reserve men are not here yet. Suppose you go and give them a whistle, Sam.'

'I don't half like leaving you,' returned Sam. 'This learned gentleman here is rather a shifty sort of chap, and it strikes me that two of us isn't a bit too much to watch him.'

'What's that?' exclaimed Sam's comrade, suspiciously.

A crash of broken crockery in the lower part of the house had followed that last word of the cautious officer's speech. Naturally, I could draw no special inference from the sound; but, for all that, it filled me with a breathless interest and suspicion, which held me irresistibly at the peephole – though the moment before I had made up my mind to fly from the house.

'Moses is awkward as well as lazy,' said the doctor. 'He has dropped the tray! Oh, dear, dear me! he has certainly dropped the tray.'

'Let's take our learned friend downstairs between us,' suggested Sam. 'I shan't be easy till we've got him out of the house.'

'And I shan't be easy if we don't handcuff him before we leave the room,' returned the other.

'Rude conduct, gentlemen – after all that has passed, remarkably rude conduct,' said the doctor. 'May I, at least, get my hat while my hands are at liberty? It hangs on that peg opposite to us.' He moved toward it a few steps into the middle of the room while he spoke.

'Stop!' said Sam. 'I'll get your hat for you. We'll see if there's anything inside it or not, before you put it on.'

The doctor stood stock-still, like a soldier at the word, Halt.

'And I'll get the handcuffs,' said the other runner, searching his coat pockets.

The doctor bowed to him assentingly and forgivingly.

'Only oblige me with my hat, and I shall be quite ready for you,' he said – paused for one moment, then repeated the words, 'Quite ready,' in a louder tone – and instantly disappeared through the floor!

I saw the two officers rush from opposite ends of the room to a great opening in the middle of it. The trapdoor on which the doctor had been standing, and on which he had descended, closed up with a bang at the same moment, and a friendly voice from the lower regions called out gaily, 'Goodbye!'

The officers next made for the door of the room. It had been locked from the other side. As they tore furiously at the handle, the roll of the wheels of the doctor's gig sounded on the drive in front of the house, and the friendly voice called out once more, 'Goodbye!'

I waited just long enough to see the baffled officers unbarring the window shutters for the purpose of giving the alarm, before I closed the peephole, and with a farewell look at the distorted face of my prostrate enemy, Screw, left the room.

The doctor's study door was open as I passed it on my way downstairs. The locked writing-desk, which probably contained the only clue to Alicia's retreat that I was likely to find, was in its usual place on the table. There was no time to break it open on the spot. I rolled it up in my apron, took it off bodily under my arm, and descended to the iron door on the staircase. Just as I was within sight of it, it was opened from the landing on the other side. I turned to run upstairs again, when a familiar voice cried, 'Stop!' and looking round, I beheld Young File.

'All right!' he said. 'Father's off with the governor in the gig, and the runners in hiding outside are in full cry after them. If Bow Street can get within pistol-shot of the blood mare, all I can say is, I give Bow Street full leave to fire away with both barrels! Where's Screw?'

'Gagged by me in the casting-room.'

'Well done, you! Got all your things, I see, under your arm? Wait two seconds while I grab my money. Never mind the rumpus upstairs – there's nobody outside to help them, and the gate's locked, if there was.'

He darted past me up the stairs. I could hear the imprisoned officers shouting for help from the top windows. Their reserve men must have been far away, by this time, in pursuit of the gig, and there was not much chance of their getting useful help from any stray countryman who might be passing along the road, except in the way of sending a message to Barkingham. Anyhow we were sure of a half-hour to escape in, at the very least.

'Now then,' said Young File, rejoining me, 'let's be off by the back way through the plantations. How came you to lay your lucky hands on Screw?' he continued, when we had passed through the iron door, and had closed it after us.

'Tell me first how the doctor managed to make a hole in the floor just in the nick of time.'

'What! did you see the trap sprung?'

'I saw everything.'

'The devil you did! Had you any notion that signals were going on, all the while you were on the watch? We have a regular set of them in case of accidents. It's a rule that father, and me, and the doctor are never to be in the workroom together – so as to keep one of us always at liberty to act on the signals. Where are you going to?'

'Only to get the gardener's ladder to help us over the wall. Go on.'

'The first signal is a private bell – that means, *Listen at the pipe*. The next is a call down the pipe for "Moses" – that means, *Danger! Lock the door*. "Stilton cheese" means, *Put the Mare to*; and "old Madeira" *Stand by the trap*. The trap works in that locked-up room you never got into, and when our hands are on the machinery, we are awkward enough to have a little accident with the luncheon tray. "Quite ready" is the signal to lower the trap, which we do in the regular theatre-fashion. We lowered the doctor smartly enough, as you saw, and got out by the back staircase. Father went in the gig, and I let them out and locked the gates after them. Now you know as much as I've got breath to tell you.'

We scaled the wall easily by the help of the ladder. When we were down on the other side, Young File suggested that the safest course for us was to separate, and for each to take his own way. We shook hands and parted. He went southward, toward London, and I went westward, toward the sea-coast, with Dr Dulcifer's precious writing-desk safe under my arm.

XII

For a couple of hours I walked on briskly, careless in what dir-ection I went, so long as I kept my back turned on Barkingham.

By the time I had put seven miles of ground, according to my calculations, between me and the red-brick house, I began to look upon the doctor's writing-desk rather in the light of an encumbrance, and determined to examine it without fur-ther delay. Accordingly I picked up the first large stone I could find in the road, crossed a common, burst through a hedge, and came to a halt, on the other side, in a thick wood. Here, finding myself well screened from public view, I broke open the desk with the help of the stone, and began to look over the contents.

To my unspeakable disappointment I found but few papers of any kind to examine. The desk was beautifully fitted with all the necessary materials for keeping up a large correspondence, but there were not more than half a dozen letters in it al-together. Four were on business matters, and the other two were of a friendly nature, referring to persons and things in which I did not feel the smallest interest. I found besides half a dozen bills receipted (the doctor was a mirror of punctuality in the payment of tradesmen), note- and letter paper of the finest quality, clarified pens, a pretty little pincushion, two small account-books filled with the neatest entries, and some leaves of blotting paper. Nothing else, absolutely nothing else, in the treacherous writing-desk on which I had implicitly relied to guide me to Alicia's hiding-place.

I groaned in sheer wretchedness over the destruction of all my dearest plans and hopes. If the Bow Street runners had come into the plantation just as I had completed the rifling of the desk I think I should have let them take me without making the slightest effort at escape. As it was, no living soul appeared within sight of me. I must have sat at the foot of a tree for full half an hour, with the doctor's useless bills and letters before me, with my head in my hands, and with all my energies of body and mind utterly crushed by despair.

At the end of the half-hour, the natural restlessness of my faculties began to make itself felt.

Whatever may be said about it in books, no emotion in this world ever did, or ever will, last for long together. The strong feeling may return over and over again, but it must have its constant intervals of change or repose. In real life the bitterest grief doggedly takes its rest and dries its eyes; the heaviest despair sinks to a certain level, and stops there to give hope a chance of rising, in spite of us. Even the joy of an unexpected meeting is always an imperfect sensation, for it never lasts long enough to justify our secret anticipations – our happiness dwindles to mere everyday contentment before we have half done with it.

I raised my head, and gathered the bills and letters together, and stood up a man again, wondering at the variableness of my own temper, at the curious elasticity of that toughest of all the vital substances within us, which we call hope. 'Sitting and sighing at the foot of this tree,' I thought, 'is not the way to find Alicia, or to secure my own safety. Let me circulate my blood and rouse my ingenuity, by taking to the road again.'

Before I forced my way back to the open side of the hedge, I thought it desirable to tear up the bills and letters, for fear of being traced by them if they were found in the plantation. The desk I left where it was, there being no name on it. The notepaper and pens I pocketed – forlorn as my situation was, it did not authorise me to waste stationery. The blotting paper was the last thing left to dispose of: two neatly folded sheets, quite clean, except in one place, where the impression of a few lines of writing appeared. I was about to put the blotting paper into my pocket after the pens, when something in the look of the writing impressed on it stopped me.

Four blurred lines appeared of not more than two or three words each, running out one beyond another regularly from left to right. Had the doctor been composing poetry and blotting it in a violent hurry? At a first glance, that was more than I could tell. The order of the written letters, whatever they might be, was reversed on the face of the impression taken of them by the blotting paper. I turned to the other side of the leaf. The order of the letters was now right, but the letters themselves were sometimes too faintly impressed, sometimes too much blurred together to be legible. I held the leaf up to the light – and there was a complete change: the blurred letters grew clearer, the invisible connecting lines appeared – I could read the words from first to last.

The writing must have been hurried, and it had to all appearance been hurriedly dried toward the corner of a perfectly clean leaf of the blotting paper. After twice reading, I felt sure that I had made out correctly the following address:

Miss Giles, 2 Zion Place, Crickgelly, N. Wales.

It was hard under the circumstances to form an opinion as to the handwriting, but I thought I could recognise the character of some of the doctor's letters, even in the blotted impression of them. Supposing I was right, who was Miss Giles?

Some Welsh friend of the doctor's, unknown to me? Probably enough. But why not Alicia herself under an assumed name? Having sent her from home to keep her out of my way, it seemed next to a certainty that her father would take all possible measures to prevent my tracing her, and would, therefore, as a common act of precaution, forbid her to travel under her own name. Crickgelly, North Wales, was assuredly a very remote place to banish her to, but then the doctor was not a man to do things by halves: he knew the lengths to which my cunning and resolution were capable of carrying me, and he would have been innocent indeed if he had hidden his daughter from me in any place within reasonable distance of Barkingham. Last, and not least important, Miss Giles sounded in my ears exactly like an assumed name.

Was there ever any woman absolutely and literally named Miss Giles? However I may have altered my opinion on this point since, my mind was not in a condition at that time to admit the possible existence of any such individual as a maiden Giles. Before, therefore, I had put the precious blotting paper into my pocket, I had satisfied myself that my first duty, under all the circumstances, was to shape my flight immediately to Crickgelly. I could be certain of nothing – not even of identifying the doctor's handwriting by the impression on the blotting paper. But provided I kept clear of Barkingham, it was all the same to me what part of the United Kingdom I went to, and, in the absence of any actual clue to her place of residence, there was consolation and encouragement even in following an imaginary trace. My spirits rose to their natural height as I struck into the high road again, and beheld across the level plain the smoke, chimneys, and church spires of a large manu-facturing town. There I saw the welcome promise of a coach – the happy chance of making my journey to Crickgelly easy and rapid from the very outset.

On my way to the town, I was reminded by the staring of all the people I passed on the road of one important consideration that I had hitherto most unaccountably overlooked – the necessity of making some radical change in my personal appearance.

I had no cause to dread the Bow Street runners, for not one of them had seen me, but I had the strongest possible reasons for distrusting a meeting with my enemy, Screw. He would certainly be made use of by the officers for the purpose of identifying the companions whom he had betrayed, and I had the best reasons in the world to believe that he would rather assist in the taking of me than in the capture of all the rest of the coining gang put together – the doctor himself not excepted. My present costume was of the dandy sort – rather shabby, but gay in colour and outrageous in cut. I had not altered it for an artisan's suit in the doctor's house, because I never had any intention of staying there a day longer than I could possibly help. The apron in which I had wrapped the writing-desk was the only approach I had made toward wearing the honourable uniform of the working man.

Would it be wise now to make my transformation complete, by adding to the apron a velveteen jacket and a sealskin cap? No: my hands were too white, my manners too inveterately gentleman-like, for all artisan disguise. It would be safer to assume a serious character – to shave off my whiskers, crop my hair, buy a modest hat and umbrella, and dress entirely in black. At the first slopshop I encountered in the suburbs of the town, I got a carpet bag and a clerical-looking suit. At the first easy shaving shop I passed, I had my hair cropped and my whiskers taken off. After that I retreated again to the country – walked back till I found a convenient hedge down a lane off the high road – changed my upper garments behind it, and emerged, bashful, black, and reverend, with my cotton umbrella tucked modestly under my arm, my eyes on the ground, my head in the air, and my hat off my forehead. When I found two labourers touching their caps to me on my way back to the town, I knew that it was all right, and that I might now set the vindictive eyes of Screw himself safely at defiance.

I had not the most distant notion where I was when I reached the High Street, and stopped at The Green Bull Hotel and Coach-office. However, I managed to mention my modest wishes to be conveyed at once in the direction of Wales, with no more than a becoming confusion of manner.

The answer was not so encouraging as I could have wished. The coach to Shrewsbury had left an hour before, and there would be no other public conveyance running in my direction until the next morning. Finding myself thus obliged to yield to adverse circumstances, I submitted resignedly, and booked a place outside by the next day's coach, in the name of the Reverend John Jones. I thought it desirable to be at once unassuming and Welsh in the selection of a travelling name, and therefore considered John Jones calculated to fit me, in my present emergency, to a hair.

After securing a bed at the hotel, and ordering a frugal curate's dinner (bit of fish, two chops, mashed potatoes, semolina pudding, half-pint of sherry), I sallied out to look at the town.

Not knowing the name of it, and not daring to excite surprise by asking, I found the place full of vague yet mysterious interest. Here I was, somewhere in central England, just as ignorant of localities as if I had been suddenly deposited in central Africa. My lively fancy revelled in the new sensation. I invented a name for the town, a code of laws for the inhabitants, productions, antiquities, chalybeate springs, population, statistics of crime, and so on, while I walked about the streets, looked in at the shop windows, and attentively examined the marketplace and town hall. Experienced travellers, who have exhausted all novelties, would do well to follow my example;

they may be certain, for one day at least, of getting some fresh ideas, and feeling a new sensation.

On returning to dinner in the coffee room, I found all the London papers on the table.

The *Morning Post* happened to lie uppermost, so I took it away to my own seat to occupy the time, while my unpretending bit of fish was frying. Glancing lazily at the advertisements on the first page, to begin with, I was astonished by the appearance of the following lines, at the top of a column:

If F—K S—FTL—Y will communicate with his distressed and alarmed relatives, Mr and Mrs B—TT—RB—RY, he will hear of something to his advantage, and may be assured that all will be once more forgiven. A—B—LLA entreats him to write.

What, in the name of all that is most mysterious, does this mean! was my first thought after reading the advertisement. Can Lady Malkinshaw have taken a fresh lease of that impregnable vital tenement, at the door of which death has been knocking vainly for so many years past? (Nothing more likely.) Was my felonious connection with Dr Dulcifer suspected? (It seemed improbable.) One thing, however, was certain: I was missed, and the Batterburys were naturally anxious about me – anxious enough to advertise in the public papers.

I debated with myself whether I should answer their pathetic appeal or not. I had all my money about me (having never let it out of my own possession during my stay in the red-brick house), and there was plenty of it for the present; so I thought it best to leave the alarm and distress of my anxious relatives unrelieved for a little while longer, and to return quietly to the perusal of the *Morning Post*.

Five minutes of desultory reading brought me unexpectedly to an explanation of the advertisement, in the shape of the following paragraph:

ALARMING ILLNESS OF LADY MALKINSHAW. – We regret to announce that this venerable lady was seized with an alarming illness on Saturday last, at her mansion in town. The attack took the character of a fit – of what precise nature we have not been able to learn. Her ladyship's medical attendant and near relative, Dr Softly, was immediately called in, and predicted the most fatal results. Fresh medical attendance was secured, and her ladyship's nearest surviving relatives, Mrs Softly, and Mr and Mrs Batterbury, of Duskydale Park, were summoned. At the time of their arrival her ladyship's condition was comatose, her breathing being highly stertorous. If we are rightly informed, Dr Softly and the other medical gentlemen present gave it as their opinion that if the pulse of the venerable sufferer did not rally in the course of a quarter of an hour at most, very lamentable results might be anticipated. For fourteen minutes, as our reporter was informed, no change took place; but, strange to relate, immediately afterward her ladyship's pulse rallied suddenly in the most extraordinary manner. She was observed to open her eyes very wide, and was heard, to the surprise and delight of all surrounding the couch, to ask why her ladyship's usual lunch of chicken broth with a glass of amontillado sherry was not placed on the table as usual. These refreshments having been pro-duced, under the sanction of the medical gentlemen, the aged patient partook of them with an appearance of the utmost relish. Since this happy alteration for the better, her ladyship's health has, we rejoice to say, rapidly improved; and the answer now given to all friendly and fashionable enquirers is, in the venerable lady's own humorous phraseology, 'Much better than could be expected.'

Well done, my excellent grandmother! my firm, my unwearied, my undying friend! Never can I say that my case is desperate while you can swallow your chicken broth and sip your amontillado sherry. The moment I want money, I will write to Mr Batterbury, and cut another little golden slice out of that possible three-thousand-pound-cake, for which he has already suffered and sacrificed so much. In the meantime, O venerable protectress of the wandering Rogue! let me gratefully drink your health in the nastiest and smallest half-pint of sherry this palate ever tasted, or these eyes ever beheld!

I went to bed that night in great spirits. My luck seemed to be returning to me, and I began to feel more than hopeful of really discovering my beloved Alicia at Crickgelly, under the alias of Miss Giles.

The next morning the Revd. John Jones descended to breakfast so rosy, bland, and smiling, that the chambermaids simpered as he tripped by them in the passage, and the landlady bowed graciously as he passed her parlour door. The coach drove up, and the reverend gentleman (after waiting characteristically for the woman's ladder) mounted to his place on the roof, behind the coachman. One man sat there who had got up before him – and who should that man be, but the chief of the Bow Street runners, who had rashly tried to take Dr Dulcifer into custody!

There could not be the least doubt of his identity; I should have known his face again among a hundred. He looked at me as I took my place by his side, with one sharp searching glance – then turned his head away toward the road. Knowing that he had never set eyes on my face (thanks to the convenient peephole at the red-brick house), I thought my meeting with him was likely to be rather advantageous than otherwise. I had now an opportunity of watching the proceedings of one of our pursuers, at any rate – and surely this was something gained.

'Fine morning, sir,' I said politely.

'Yes,' he replied in the gruffest of monosyllables.

I was not offended: I could make allowance for the feelings of a man who had been locked up by his own prisoner.

'Very fine morning, indeed,' I repeated, soothingly and cheerfully.

The runner only grunted this time. Well, well! we all have our little infirmities. I don't think the worse of the man now, for having been rude to me, that morning, on the top of the Shrewsbury coach.

The next passenger who got up and placed himself by my side was a florid, excitable, confused-looking gentleman, excessively talkative and familiar. He was followed by a sulky agricultural youth in top boots – and then, the complement of passengers on our seat behind the coachman was complete.

'Heard the news, sir?' said the florid man, turning to me.

'Not that I am aware of,' I answered.

'It's the most tremendous thing that has happened these fifty years,' said the florid man. 'A gang of coiners, sir, discovered at Barkingham – in a house they used to call the Grange. All the dreadful lot of bad silver that's been about, they're at the bottom of. And the head of the gang not taken! Escaped, sir, like a ghost on the stage, through a trapdoor, after actually locking the runners into his workshop. The blacksmiths from Barkingham had to break them out; the whole house was found full of iron doors, back staircases, and all that sort of thing, just like the Inquisition. A most respectable man, the original proprietor! Think what a misfortune to have let his house to a scoundrel who has turned the whole inside into traps, furnaces, and iron doors. The fellow's reference, sir, was actually at a London bank, where he kept a first-rate account. What is to become of society? Where is our protection? Where are our characters, when we are left at the mercy of scoundrels? The times are awful – upon my soul, the times we live in are perfectly awful!'

'Pray, sir, is there any chance of catching this coiner?' I enquired innocently.

'I hope so, sir; for the sake of outraged society, I hope so,' said the excitable man. 'They've printed handbills at Barkingham, offering a reward for taking him. I was with my friend the mayor, early this morning, and saw them issued. "Mr Mayor," says I, "I'm going west – give me a few copies – let me help to circulate them – for the sake of outraged society, let me help to circulate them." Here they are – take a few, sir, for distribution. You'll see these are three other fellows to be caught besides the principal rascal – one of them a scamp belonging to a respectable family. Oh! what times! Take three copies, and pray circulate them in three influential quarters. Perhaps that gentleman next you would like a few. Will you take three, sir?'

'No, I won't,' said the Bow Street runner doggedly. 'Nor yet one of 'em – and it's my opinion that the coining-gang would be nabbed all the sooner, if you was to give over helping the law to catch them.'

This answer produced a vehement expostulation from my excitable neighbour, to which I paid little attention, being better engaged in reading the handbill.

It described the doctor's personal appearance with remarkable accuracy, and cautioned persons in seaport towns to be on the lookout for him. Old File, Young File, and myself were all dishonourably mentioned together in a second paragraph, as runaways of inferior importance Not a word was said in the handbill to show that the authorities at Barkingham even so much as suspected the direction in which any one of us had escaped. This would have been very encouraging, but for the presence of the runner by my side, which looked as if Bow Street had its suspicions, however innocent Barkingham might be.

Could the doctor have directed his flight toward Crickgelly? I trembled internally as the question suggested itself to me. Surely he would prefer writing to Miss Giles to join him when he got to a safe place of refuge, rather than encumber himself with the young lady before he was well out of reach of the far-stretching arm of the law. This seemed infinitely the most natural course of conduct. Still, there was the runner travelling toward Wales – and not certainly without a special motive. I put the handbills in my pocket, and listened for any hints that might creep out in his talk, but he perversely kept silent. The more my excitable neighbour tried to dispute with him, the more contemptuously he refused to break silence. I began to feel vehemently impatient for our arrival at Shrewsbury, for there only could I hope to discover something more of my formidable fellow-traveller's plans.

The coach stopped for dinner, and some of our passengers left us, the excitable man with the handbills among the number. I got down, and stood on the doorstep of the inn, pretending to be looking about me, but in reality watching the movements of the runner.

Rather to my surprise, I saw him go to the door of the coach and speak to one of the inside passengers. After a short conversation, of which I could not hear one word, the runner left the coach door and entered the inn, called for a glass of brandy and water, and took it out to his friend, who had not left the vehicle. The friend bent forward to receive it at the window. I caught a glimpse of his face, and felt my knees tremble under me – it was Screw himself!

Screw, pale and haggard-looking, evidently not yet recovered from the effect of my grip on his throat! Screw, in attendance on the runner, travelling inside the coach in the character of an invalid. He must be going this journey to help the Bow Street officers to identify some one of our scattered gang of whom they were in pursuit. It could not be the doctor – the runner could discover him without assistance from anybody. Why might it not be me?

I began to think whether it would be best to trust boldly in my disguise, and my lucky position outside the coach, or whether I should abandon my fellow-passengers immediately. It was not easy to settle at once which course was the safest – so I tried the effect of looking at my two alternatives from another point of view. Should I risk everything, and go on resolutely to Crickgelly, on the chance of discovering that Alicia and Miss Giles were one and the same person – or should I give up on the spot the only prospect of finding my lost mistress, and direct my attention entirely to the business of looking after my own safety?

As the latter alternative practically resolved itself into the simple question of whether I should act like a man who was in love, or like a man who was not, my natural instincts settled the difficulty in no time. I boldly imitated the example of my fellow-passengers, and went in to dinner, determined to go on afterward to Crickgelly, though all Bow Street should be following at my heels.

XIII

Secure as I tried to feel in my change of costume, my cropped hair, and my whiskerless cheeks, I kept well away from the coach-window, when the dinner at the inn was over and the passengers were called to take their places again. Thus far – thanks to the strength of my grasp on his neck, which had left him too weak to be an outside passenger – Screw had certainly not seen me, and, if I played my cards properly, there was no reason why he should see me before we got to our destination.

Throughout the rest of the journey I observed the strictest caution, and fortune seconded my efforts. It was dark when we got to Shrewsbury. On leaving the coach I was enabled, under cover of the night, to keep a sharp watch on the proceedings of Screw and his Bow Street ally. They did not put up at the hotel, but walked away to a public house. There, my clerical character obliged me to leave them at the door.

I returned to the hotel, to make enquiries about conveyances.

The answers informed me that Crickgelly was a little fishing village, and that there was no coach direct to it, but that two coaches running to two small Welsh towns situated at nearly equal distances from my destination, on either side of it, would pass through Shrewsbury the next morning. The waiter added, that I could book a place – conditionally – by either of these vehicles, and that, as they were always well-filled, I had better be quick in making my choice between them. Matters had now arrived at such a pass, that nothing was left for me but to trust to chance. If I waited till the morning to see whether Screw and the Bow Street runner travelled in my direction, and to find out, in case they did, which coach they took, I should be running the risk of losing a place for myself, and so delaying my journey for another day. This was not to be thought of. I told the waiter to book me a place in which coach he pleased. The two were called respectively the Humming Bee, and the Red Cross Knight. The waiter chose the latter.

Sleep was not much in my way that night. I rose almost as early as Boots himself – breakfasted – then sat at the coffee-room window looking out anxiously for the two coaches.

Nobody seemed to agree which would pass first. Each of the inn servants of whom I enquired made it a matter of partisanship, and backed his favourite coach with the most consummate assurance. At last, I heard the guard's horn and the clatter of the horses' hoofs. Up drove a coach – I looked out cautiously – it was the Humming Bee. Three outside places were vacant: one behind the coachman, two on the dicky. The first was taken immediately by a farmer, the second – to my unspeakable disgust and terror – was secured by the inevitable Bow Street runner, who, as soon as he was up, helped the weakly Screw into the third place, by his side. They were going to Crickgelly; not a doubt of it, now.

I grew mad with impatience for the arrival of the Red Cross Knight. Half an hour passed – forty minutes – and then I heard another horn and another clatter – and the Red Cross Knight rattled up to the hotel door at full speed. What if there should be no vacant place for me! I ran to the door with a sinking heart. Outside, the coach was declared to be full.

'There is one inside place,' said the waiter, 'if you don't mind paying the – '

Before he could say the rest, I was occupying that one inside place. I remember nothing of the journey from the time we left the hotel door, except that it was fearfully long. At some hour of the day with which I was not acquainted (for my watch had stopped for want of winding up), I was set down in a clean little street of a prim little town (the name of which I never thought of asking), and was told that the coach never went any further.

No post-chaise was to be had. With incredible difficulty I got first a gig, then a man to drive it, and, last, a pony to draw it. We hobbled away crazily from the inn door. I thought of Screw and the Bow Street runner approaching Crickgelly, from their point of the compass, perhaps at the full speed of a good post-chaise – I thought of that, and would have given all the money in my pocket for two hours' use of a fast road-hack.

Judging by the time we occupied in making the journey, and a little also by my own impatience, I should say that Crickgelly must have been at least twenty miles distant from the town where I took the gig. The sun was setting when we first heard, through the evening stillness, the sound of the surf on the seashore. The twilight was falling as we entered the little fishing village, and let our unfortunate pony stop, for the last time, at a small inn door.

The first question I asked of the landlord was, whether two gentlemen (friends of mine, of course, whom I expected to meet) had driven into Crickgelly, a little while before me. The reply was in the negative, and the sense of relief it produced seemed to rest me at once, body and mind, after my long and anxious journey. Either I had beaten the spies on the road, or they were not bound to Crickgelly. Anyway, I had first possession of the field of action. I paid the man who had driven me, and asked my way to Zion Place. My directions were simple – I had only to go through the village, and I should find Zion Place at the other end of it.

The village had a very strong smell, and a curious habit of building boats in the street between intervals of detached cottages; a helpless, muddy, fishy little place. I walked through it rapidly; turned inland a few hundred yards; ascended some rising ground; and discerned, in the dim twilight, four small lonesome villas standing in pairs, with a shed and a saw-pit on one side, and a few shells of unfinished houses on the other. Some madly speculative builder was evidently trying to turn Crickgelly into a watering-place.

I made out number two, and discovered the bell-handle with difficulty, it was growing so dark. A servant-maid – corporeally enormous, but, as I soon found, in a totally undeveloped state, mentally – opened the door.

'Does Miss Giles live here?' I asked.

'Don't see no visitors,' answered the large maiden. 'T'other one tried it and had to go away. You go, too.'

'T'other one?' I repeated. 'Another visitor? And when did he call?'

'Better than an hour ago.'

'Was there nobody with him?'

'No. Don't see no visitors. He went. You go, too.'

Just as she repeated that exasperating formula of words, a door opened at the end of the passage. My voice had evidently reached the ears of somebody in the back parlour. Who the person was I could not see, but I heard the rustle of a woman's dress. My situation was growing desperate, my suspicions were aroused – I determined to risk everything – and I called softly in the direction of the open door, 'Alicia!'

A voice answered, 'Good heavens! Frank?' It was *her* voice. She had recognised mine. I pushed past the big servant; in two steps I was at the end of the passage; in one more I was in the back parlour.

She was there, standing alone by the side of a table. Seeing my changed costume and altered face, she turned deadly pale, and stretched her hand behind her mechanically, as if to take hold of a chair. I caught her in my arms, but I was afraid to kiss her – she trembled so when I only touched her.

'Frank!' she said, drawing her head back. 'What is it? How did you find out? For mercy's sake what does it mean?'

'It means, love, that I've come to take care of you for the rest of your life and mine, if you will only let me. Don't tremble – there's nothing to be afraid of! Only compose yourself, and I'll tell you why I am here in this strange disguise. Come, come, Alicia! Don't look like that at me. You called me Frank just now, for the first time. Would you have done that, if you had disliked me or forgotten me?'

I saw her colour beginning to come back – the old bright glow returning to the dear, dusky cheeks. If I had not seen them so near me, I might have exercised some self-control – as it was, I lost my presence of mind entirely, and kissed her.

She drew herself away half-frightened, half-confused – certainly not offended, and, apparently, not very likely to faint – which was more than I could have said of her when I first entered the room. Before she had time to reflect on the peril and awkwardness of our position, I pressed the first necessary questions on her rapidly, one after the other.

'Where is Mrs Baggs?' I asked first.

Mrs Baggs was the housekeeper.

Alicia pointed to the closed folding doors. 'In the front parlour, asleep on the sofa.'

'Have you any suspicion who the stranger was who called more than an hour ago?'

'None. The servant told him we saw no visitors, and he went away, without leaving his name.'

'Have you heard from your father?'

She began to turn pale again, but controlled herself bravely, and answered in a whisper: 'Mrs Baggs had a short note from him this morning. It was not dated, and it only said circumstances had happened that obliged him to leave home suddenly, and that we were to wait here till be wrote again, most likely in a few days.'

'Now, Alicia,' I said, as lightly as I could, 'I have the highest possible opinion of your courage, good sense, and self-control, and I shall expect you to keep up your reputation in my eyes, while you are listening to what I have to tell you.'

Saying these words, I took her by the hand and made her sit close by me; then, breaking it to her as gently and gradually as possible, I told her all that had happened at the red-brick house since the evening when she left the dinner table and we exchanged our parting look at the dining-room door.

It was almost as great a trial to me to speak as it was to her to hear. She suffered so violently, felt such evident misery of shame and terror while I was relating the strange events that had occurred in her absence, that I once or twice stopped in alarm, and almost repented my boldness in telling her the truth. However, fair dealing with her, cruel as it might seem at the time, was the best and safest course for the future. How could I expect her to put all her trust in me if I began by deceiving her – if I fell into prevarications and excuses at the very outset of our renewal of intercourse? I went on desperately to the end, taking a hopeful view of the most hopeless circumstances, and making my narrative as mercifully short as possible.

When I had done, the poor girl, in the extremity of her forlornness and distress, forgot all the little maidenly conventionalities and young-lady-like restraints of everyday life – and, in a burst of natural grief and honest confiding helplessness, hid her face on my bosom, and cried there as if she were a child again, and I was the mother to whom she had been used to look for comfort.

I made no attempt to stop her tears – they were the safest and best vent for the violent agitation under which she was suffering. I said nothing; words, at such a time as that, would only have aggravated her distress. All the questions I had to ask, all the proposals I had to make, must, I felt, be put off – no matter at what risk – until some later and calmer hour. There we sat together, with one long-unsnuffed candle lighting us smokily; with the discordantly grotesque sound of the house-keeper's snoring in the front room, mingling with the sobs of the weeping girl on my bosom. No other noise, great or small, inside the house or out of it, was audible. The summer night looked black and cloudy through the little back window.

I was not much easier in my mind now that the trial of breaking my bad news to Alicia was over. That stranger who had called at the house an hour before me weighed on my spirits. It could not have been Dr Dulcifer. He would have gained admission. Could it be the Bow Street runner, or Screw? I had lost sight of them, it is true, but had they lost sight of me?

Alicia's grief gradually exhausted itself. She feebly raised her head, and, turning it away from me, hid her face. I saw that she was not fit for talking yet, and begged her to go upstairs to the drawing room and lie down a little. She looked apprehensively toward the folding doors that shut us off from the front parlour.

'Leave Mrs Baggs to me,' I said. 'I want to have a few words with her, and, as soon as you are gone, I'll make noise enough here to wake her.'

Alicia looked at me enquiringly and amazedly. I did not speak again. Time was now of terrible importance to us – I gently led her to the door.

XIV

As soon as I was alone, I took from my pocket one of the handbills that my excitable fellow-traveller had presented to me, so as to have it ready for Mrs Baggs the moment we stood face to face. Armed with this ominous letter of introduction, I kicked a chair down against the folding doors, by way of giving a preliminary knock to arouse the housekeeper's attention. The plan was immediately successful. Mrs Baggs opened the doors of communication violently. A slight smell of spirits entered the room, and was followed close by the housekeeper herself, with an indignant face and a disordered headdress.

'What do you mean, sir? How dare you – ' she began, then stopped aghast, looking at me in speechless astonishment.

'I have been obliged to make a slight alteration in my personal appearance, ma'am,' I said. 'But I am still Frank Softly.'

'Don't talk to me about personal appearances, sir,' cried Mrs Baggs recovering. 'What do you mean by being here? Leave the house immediately. I shall write to the doctor, Mr Softly, this very night.'

'He has no address you can direct to,' I rejoined. 'If you don't believe me, read that.' I gave her the handbill without another word of preface.

Mrs Baggs looked at it – lost in an instant some of the fine colour plentifully diffused over her face by sleep and spirits – sat down in the nearest chair with a thump that seemed to threaten the very foundations of number two, Zion Place – and stared me hard in the face, the most speechless and helpless elderly female I ever beheld.

'Take plenty of time to compose yourself ma'am,' I said. 'If you don't see the doctor again soon, under the gallows, you will probably not have the pleasure of meeting with him for some considerable time.'

Mrs Baggs smote both her hands distractedly on her knees, and whispered a devout ejaculation to herself softly.

'Allow me to deal with you, ma'am, as a woman of the world,' I went on. 'If you will give me half an hour's hearing, I will explain to you how I come to know what I do, how I got here, and what I have to propose to Miss Alicia and to you.'

'If you have the feelings of a man, sir,' said Mrs Baggs, shaking her head and raising her eyes to heaven, 'you will remember that I have nerves, and will not presume upon them.'

As the old lady uttered the last words, I thought I saw her eyes turn from heaven, and take the earthly direction of the sofa in the front parlour. It struck me also that her lips looked rather dry. Upon these two hints I spoke.

'Might I suggest some little stimulant?' I asked, with respectful earnestness. 'I have heard my grandmother (Lady Malkinshaw) say that, "a drop in time saves nine".'

'You will find it under the sofa pillow,' said Mrs Baggs, with sudden briskness. ' "A drop in time saves nine" – my sentiments, if I may put myself on a par with her ladyship. The liqueur glass, Mr Softly, is in the backgammon board. I hope her ladyship was well the last time you heard from her? Suffers from her nerves, does she? Like me, again. In the backgammon board. Oh, this news, this awful news!'

I found the bottle of brandy in the place indicated, but no liqueur glass in the backgammon board. There was, however, a wine glass, accidentally left on a chair by the sofa. Mrs Baggs did not seem to notice the difference when I brought it into the back room and filled it with brandy.

'Take a toothful yourself,' said Mrs Baggs, lightly tossing off the dram in a moment. ' "A drop in time" – I can't help repeating it, it's so nicely expressed. Still, with submission to her ladyship's better judgment, Mr Softly, the question seems now to arise, whether, if one drop in time saves nine, two drops in time may not save eighteen.' Here Mrs Baggs forgot her nerves and winked. I returned the wink and filled the glass a second time. 'Oh, this news, this awful news!' said Mrs Baggs, remembering her nerves again.

Just then I thought I heard footsteps in front of the house, but, listening more attentively, found that it had begun to rain, and that I had been deceived by the pattering of the first heavy drops against the windows. However, the bare suspicion that the same stranger who had called already might be watching the house now was enough to startle me very seriously, and to suggest the absolute necessity of occupying no more precious time in paying attention to the vagaries of Mrs Baggs' nerves. It was also of some importance that I should speak to her while she was sober enough to understand what I meant in a general way.

Feeling convinced that she was in imminent danger of becoming downright drunk if I gave her another glass, I kept my hand on the bottle, and forthwith told my story over again in a very abridged and unceremonious form, and without allowing her one moment of leisure for comment on my narrative, whether it might be of the weeping, winking, drinking, groaning, or ejaculating kind. As I had anticipated, when I came to a conclusion and consequently allowed her an opportunity of saying a few words, she affected to be extremely shocked and surprised at hearing of the nature of her master's pursuits, and reproached me in terms of the most vehement and virtuous indignation for incurring the guilt of abetting them, even though I had done so from the very excusable motive of saving my own life. Having a lively sense of the humorous, I was necessarily rather amused by this; but I began to get a little surprised as well, when we diverged to the subject of the doctor's escape, on finding that Mrs Baggs viewed the fact of his running away to some hiding place of his own in the light of a personal insult to his faithful and attached housekeeper.

'It shows a want of confidence in me,' said the old lady, 'that I may forgive, but can never forget. The sacrifices I have made for that ungrateful man are not to be told in words. The very morning he sent us away here, what did I do? Packed up the moment he said go. I had my preserves to pot, and the kitchen chimney to be swept, and the lock of my box hampered into the bargain. Other women in my place would have grumbled – I got up directly, as lively as any girl of eighteen you like to mention. Says he, "I want Alicia taken out of young Softly's way, and you must do it." – Says I, "This very morning, sir?" – Says he, "This very morning." – Says I, "Where to?" – Says he, "As far off as ever you can go: coast of Wales – Crickgelly. I won't trust her nearer; young Softly's too cunning, and she's too fond of him." – "Any more orders, sir?' says I. – "Yes; take some fancy name – Simkins, Johnson, Giles, Jones, James," says he, "what you like but Dulcifer; for that scamp Softly will move heaven and earth to trace her." – "What else?" says I. – "Nothing, but look sharp," says he; "and mind one thing, that she sees no visitors, and posts no letters." Before those last words had been out of his wicked lips an hour, we were off. A nice job I had to get her away – a nice job to stop her from writing letters to you – a nice job to keep her here. But I did it; I followed my orders like a slave in a plantation with a whip at his bare back. I've had rheumatics, weak legs, bad nights, and miss in the sulks – all from obeying the doctor's orders. And what is my reward? He turns coiner, and runs away without a word to me beforehand, and writes me a trumpery note, without a date to it, without a farthing of money in it, telling me nothing! Look at my confidence in him, and then look at the way he's treated me in return. What woman's nerves can stand that? Don't keep fidgeting with the bottle! Pass it this way, Mr Softly, or you'll break it, and drive me distracted.'

'He has no excuse, ma'am,' I said. 'But will you allow me to change the subject, as I am pressed for time? You appear to be so well acquainted with the favourable opinion that Miss Alicia and I entertain of each other that I hope it will be no fresh shock to your nerves if I inform you, in plain words, that I have come to Crickgelly to marry her.'

'Marry her! marry – If you don't leave off fidgeting with the bottle, Mr Softly, and change the subject directly, I shall ring the bell.'

'Hear me out, ma'am, and then ring if you like. If you persist, however, in considering yourself still the confidential servant of a felon who is now flying for his life, and if you decline allowing the young lady to act as she wishes, I will not be so rude as to hint that – as she is of age – she may walk out of this house with me, whenever she likes, without your having the power to prevent her; but, I will politely ask instead, what you would propose to do with her, in the straitened position as to money in which she and you are likely to be placed? You can't find her father to give her to, and, if you could, who would be the best protector for her? The doctor, who is the principal criminal in the eye of the law, or I, who am only the unwilling accomplice? He is known to the Bow Street runners – I am not. There is a reward for the taking of him, and none for the taking of me. He has no respectable relatives and friends, I have plenty. Every way my chances are the best, and consequently I am, every way, the fittest person to trust her to. Don't you see that?'

Mrs Baggs did not immediately answer. She snatched the bottle out of my hands – drank off another dram, shook her head at me, and ejaculated lamentably: 'My nerves, my nerves! what a heart of stone he must have to presume on my poor nerves!'

'Give me one minute more,' I went on. 'I propose to take you and Alicia tomorrow morning to Scotland. Pray don't groan! I only suggest the journey with a matrimonial object. In Scotland, Mrs Baggs, if a man and woman accept each other as husband and wife, before one witness, it is a lawful marriage, and that kind of wedding is, as you see plainly enough, the only safe refuge for a bridegroom in my situation. If you consent to come with us to Scotland, and serve as witness to the marriage, I shall be delighted to acknowledge my sense of your kindness in the eloquent language of the Bank of England, as expressed to the world in general on the surface of a five-pound note.'

I cautiously snatched away the brandy bottle as I spoke, and was in the drawing room with it in an instant. As I suppose, Mrs Baggs tried to follow me, for I heard the door rattle, as if she had got out of her chair, and suddenly slipped back into it again. I felt certain of her deciding to help us, if she was only sober enough to reflect on what I had said to her. The journey to Scotland was a tedious, and perhaps a dangerous, under-taking. But I had no other alternative to choose.

In those uncivilised days, the Marriage Act had not been passed, and there was no convenient hymeneal registrar in England to change a vagabond runaway couple into a respect-able man and wife at a moment's notice. The trouble and expense of taking Mrs Baggs with us, I encountered, of course, solely out of regard for Alicia's natural prejudices. She had led precisely that kind of life that makes any woman but a bad one morbidly sensitive on the subject of small proprieties. If she had been a girl with a recognised position in society, I should have proposed to her to run away with me alone. As it was, the very defencelessness of her situation gave her, in my opinion, the right to expect from me even the absurdest sacrifices to the narrowest conventionalities. Mrs Baggs was not quite so sober in her habits, perhaps, as matrons in general are expected to be, but, for my particular purpose, this was only a slight blemish; it takes so little, after all, to represent the abstract principle of propriety in the short-sighted eye of the world.

As I reached the drawing-room door, I looked at my watch.

Nine o'clock! and nothing done yet to facilitate our escaping from Crickgelly to the regions of civilised life the next morning. I was pleased to hear, when I knocked at the door, that Alicia's voice sounded firmer as she told me to come in. She was more confused than astonished or frightened when I sat down by her on the sofa, and repeated the principal topics of my conversion with Mrs Baggs.

'Now, my own love,' I said, in conclusion – suiting my gestures, it is unnecessary to say, to the tenderness of my language – 'there is not the least doubt that Mrs Baggs will end by agreeing to my proposals. Nothing remains, therefore, but for you to give me the answer now, which I have been waiting for ever since that last day when we met by the riverside. I did not know then what the motive was for your silence and distress. I know now, and I love you better after that knowledge than I did before it.'

Her head dropped into its former position on my bosom, and she murmured a few words, but too faintly for me to hear them.

'You knew more about your father, then, than I did?' I whispered.

'Less than you have told me since,' she interposed quickly, without raising her face.

'Enough to convince you that he was breaking the laws,' I suggested; 'and, to make you, as his daughter, shrink from saying "yes" to me when we sat together on the riverbank?'

She did not answer. One of her arms, which was hanging over my shoulder, stole round my neck, and clasped it gently.

'Since that time,' I went on, 'your father has compromised me. I am in some danger, not much, from the law. I have no prospects that are not of the most doubtful kind, and I have no excuse for asking you to share them, except that I have fallen into my present misfortune through trying to discover the obstacle that kept us apart. If there is any protection in the world that you can turn to, less doubtful than mine, I suppose I ought to say no more, and leave the house. But if there should be none, surely I am not so very selfish in asking you to take your chance with me? I honestly believe that I shall have little difficulty, with ordinary caution, in escaping from pursuit, and finding a safe home somewhere to begin life in again with new interests. Will you share it with me, Alicia? I can try no fresh persuasions –I have no right, perhaps, in my present situation to have addressed so many to you already.'

Her other arm stole round my neck; she laid her cheek against mine, and whispered, 'Be kind to me, Frank – I have nobody in the world who loves me but you!'

I felt her tears on my face; my own eyes moistened as I tried to answer her. We sat for some minutes in perfect silence – without moving, without a thought beyond the moment. The rising of the wind and the splashing of the rain outside were the first sounds that stirred me into action again.

I summoned my resolution, rose from the sofa, and in a few hasty words told Alicia what I proposed for the next day, and

133

mentioned the hour at which I would come in the morning. As I had anticipated, she seemed relieved and reassured at the prospect even of such slight sanction and encouragement, on the part of another woman, as would be implied by the companionship of Mrs Baggs on the journey to Scotland.

The next and last difficulty I had to encounter was necessarily connected with her father. He had never been very affectionate, and he was now, for aught she or I knew to the contrary, parted from her forever. Still, the instinctive recognition of his position made her shrink, at the last moment, when she spoke of him, and thought of the serious nature of her engagement with me. After some vain arguing and remonstrating, I contrived to quiet her scruples by promising that an address should be left at Crickgelly, to which any second letter that might arrive from the doctor could be forwarded. When I saw that this prospect of being able to communicate with him, if he wrote or wished to see her, had sufficiently composed her mind, I left the drawing room. It was vitally important that I should get back to the inn and make the necessary arrangements for our departure the next morning, before the primitive people of the place had retired to bed.

As I passed the back parlour door on my way out, I heard the voice of Mrs Baggs raised indignantly. The words 'bottle!', 'audacity!' and 'nerves!' reached my ear disjointedly. I called out 'Goodbye! till tomorrow;' heard a responsive groan of disgust, then opened the front door, and plunged out into the dark and rainy night.

It might have been the dropping of water from the cottage roofs while I passed through the village, or the groundless alarm of my own suspicious fancy, but I thought I was being followed as I walked back to the inn. Two or three times I turned round abruptly. If twenty men had been at my heels, it was too dark to see them. I went on to the inn.

The people there were not gone to bed, and I sent for the landlord to consult with him about a conveyance. Perhaps it was my suspicious fancy again, but I thought his manner was altered. He seemed half distrustful, half afraid of me, when I asked him if there had been any signs, during my absence, of those two gentlemen for whom I had already enquired on arriving at his door that evening. He gave an answer in the negative, looking away from me while he spoke.

Thinking it advisable, on the whole, not to let him see that I noticed a change in him, I proceeded at once to the question of the conveyance, and was told that I could hire the landlord's light cart, in which he was accustomed to drive to the market town. I appointed an hour for starting the next day, and retired at once to my bedroom. There my thoughts were enough. I was anxious about Screw and the Bow Street runner. I was uncertain about the stranger who had called at number two, Zion Place. I was in doubt even about the landlord of the inn. Never did I know what real suffering from suspense was until that night. Whatever my apprehensions might have been, they were none of them realised the next morning.

Nobody followed me on my way to Zion Place, and no stranger had called there before me a second time, when I made enquiries on entering the house. I found Alicia blushing, and Mrs Baggs impenetrably wrapped up in dignified sulkiness. After informing me with a lofty look that she intended to go to Scotland with us, and to take my five-pound note – partly under protest, and partly out of excessive affection for Alicia – she retired to pack up. The time consumed in performing this process, and the further delay occasioned by paying small outstanding debts to tradespeople, and settling with the owner of the house, detained us till nearly noon before we were ready to get into the landlord's cart.

I looked behind me anxiously at starting, and often afterward on the road, but never saw anything to excite my suspicions. In settling matters with the landlord overnight, I had arranged that we should be driven to the nearest town at which a post-chaise could be obtained. My resources were just as likely to hold out against the expenses of posting, where public conveyances could not be obtained, as against the expense of waiting privately at hotels until the right coaches might start. According to my calculations, my money would last till we got to Scotland. After that, I had my watch, rings, shirtpin, and Mr Batterbury, to help in replenishing my purse. Anxious, therefore, as I was about other things, money matters, for once in a way, did not cause me the smallest uneasiness.

XV

We posted five-and-thirty miles, then stopped for a couple of hours to rest, and wait for a night coach running northward.

On getting into this vehicle we were fortunate enough to find the fourth inside place not occupied. Mrs Baggs showed her sense of the freedom from restraint thus obtained by tying a huge red comforter round her head like a turban, and immediately falling fast asleep. This gave Alicia and me full liberty to talk as we pleased. Our conversation was for the most part of that particular kind that is not of the smallest importance to any third person in the whole world. One portion of it, however, was an exception to this general rule. It had a very positive influence on my fortunes, and it is, therefore, I hope, of sufficient importance to bear being communicated to the reader.

We had changed horses for the fourth time, had seated ourselves comfortably in our places, and had heard Mrs Baggs resume the kindred occupations of sleeping and snoring, when Alicia whispered to me: 'I must have no secrets, now, from you – must I, Frank?'

'You must have anything you like, do anything you like, and say anything you like. You must never ask leave – but only grant it!'

'Shall you always tell me that, Frank?'

I did not answer in words, but the conversation suffered a momentary interruption. Of what nature, susceptible people will easily imagine. As for the hard-hearted, I don't write for them.

'My secret need not alarm you,' Alicia went on, in tones that began to sound rather sadly. 'It is only about a tiny pasteboard box that I can carry in the bosom of my dress. But it has got three diamonds in it, Frank, and one beautiful ruby. Did you ever give me credit for having so much that was valuable about me? Shall I give it you to keep for me?'

I remembered directly Old File's story of Mrs Dulcifer's elopement, and of the jewels she had taken with her. It was easy to guess, after what I had heard, that the poor woman had secretly preserved some of her little property for the benefit of her child.

'I have no present need of money, darling,' I answered. 'Keep the box in its present enviable position.' I stopped there, saying nothing of the thought that was really uppermost in my mind. If any unforeseen accident placed me within the grip of the law, I should not now have the double trial to endure of leaving my wife for a prison, and leaving her helpless.

Morning dawned and found us still awake. The sun rose, Mrs Baggs left off snoring, and we arrived at the last stage before the coach stopped.

I got out to see about some tea for my travelling companions, and looked up at the outside passengers. One of them seated in the dicky looked down at me. He was a countryman in a smock-frock, with a green patch over one of his eyes. Something in the expression of his uncovered eye made me pause – reflect – turn away uneasily – and then look again at him furtively. A sudden shudder ran through me from top to toe, my heart sank, and my head began to feel giddy. The countryman in the dicky was no other than the Bow Street runner in disguise.

I kept away from the coach till the fresh horses were on the point of starting, for I was afraid to let Alicia see my face, after making that fatal discovery. She noticed how pale I was when I got in. I made the best excuse I could, and gently insisted on her trying to sleep a little after being awake all night. She lay back in her corner, and Mrs Baggs, comforted with a morning dram in her tea, fell asleep again. I had thus an hour's leisure before me to think what I should do next.

Screw was not in company with the runner this time. He must have managed to identify me somewhere, and the officer doubtless knew my personal appearance well enough now to follow and make sure of me without help. That I was the man whom he was tracking could not be doubted: his disguise and his position on the top of the coach proved it only too plainly.

But why had he not seized me at once? Probably because he had some ulterior purpose to serve, which would have been thwarted by my immediate apprehension. What that purpose was I did my best to fathom, and, as I thought, succeeded in the attempt. What I was to do when the coach stopped was a more difficult point to settle. To give the runner the slip, with two women to take care of, was simply impossible. To treat him as I had treated Screw at the red-brick house, was equally out of the question, for he was certain to give me no chance of catching him alone. To keep him in ignorance of the real object of my journey, and thereby to delay his discovering himself and attempting to make me a prisoner, seemed the only plan on the safety of which I could place the smallest reliance. If I had ever had any idea of following the example of other runaway lovers and going to Gretna Green, I should now have abandoned it. All roads in that direction would betray what the purpose of my journey was if I took them. Some large town in Scotland would be the safest destination that I could publicly advertise myself as bound for. Why not boldly say that I was going with the two ladies to Edinburgh?

Such was the plan of action that I now adopted.

To give any idea of the distracted condition of my mind at the time when I was forming it is simply impossible. As for doubting whether I ought to marry at all under these dangerous circumstances, I must frankly own that I was too selfishly and violently in love to look the question fairly in the face at first. When I subsequently forced myself to consider it, the most distinct project I could frame for overcoming all difficulty was to marry myself (the phrase is strictly descriptive of the Scottish ceremony) at the first inn we came to, over the Border; to hire a chaise, or take places in a public conveyance to Edinburgh, as a blind; to let Alicia and Mrs Baggs occupy those places; to remain behind myself; and to trust to my audacity and cunning, when left alone, to give the runner the slip. Writing of it now, in cool blood, this seems as wild and hopeless a plan as ever was imagined. But, in the confused and distracted state of all my faculties at that period, it seemed quite easy to execute, and not in the least doubtful as to any one of its probable results.

On reaching the town at which the coach stopped, we found ourselves obliged to hire another chaise for a short distance, in order to get to the starting point of a second coach. Again we took inside places, and again, at the first stages when I got down to look at the outside passengers, there was the country-man with the green shade over his eye. Whatever conveyance we travelled by on our northward road, we never escaped him. He never attempted to speak to me, never seemed to notice me, and never lost sight of me. On and on we went, over roads that seemed interminable, and still the dreadful sword of justice hung always, by its single hair, over my head. My haggard face, my feverish hands, my confused manner, my inexpressible impatience, all belied the excuses with which I desperately continued to ward off Alicia's growing fears, and Mrs Baggs' indignant suspicions. 'Oh! Frank, something has happened! For God's sake, tell me what!' – 'Mr Softly, I can see through a deal board as far as most people. You are following the doctor's wicked example, and showing a want of confidence in me.' These were the remonstrances of Alicia and the housekeeper.

At last we got out of England, and I was still a free man. The chaise (we were posting again) brought us into a dirty town, and drew up at the door of a shabby inn. A shock-headed girl received us.

'Are we in Scotland?' I asked.

'Mon! whar' else should ye be?' The accent relieved me of all doubt.

'A private room – something to eat, ready in an hour's time – chaise afterward to the nearest place from which a coach runs to Edinburgh.' Giving these orders rapidly, I followed the girl with my travelling companions into a stuffy little room. As soon as our attendant had left us, I locked the door, put the key in my pocket, and took Alicia by the hand.

'Now, Mrs Baggs,' said I, 'bear witness – '

'You're not going to marry her now!' interposed Mrs Baggs, indignantly. 'Bear witness, indeed! I won't bear witness till I've taken off my bonnet, and put my hair tidy!'

'The ceremony won't take a minute,' I answered, 'and I'll give you your five-pound note and open the door the moment it's over. Bear witness,' I went on, drowning Mrs Baggs' expostulations with the all-important marriage words, 'that I take this woman, Alicia Dulcifer, for my lawful wedded wife.'

'In sickness and in health, in poverty and wealth,' broke in Mrs Baggs, determining to represent the clergyman as well as to be the witness.

'Alicia, dear,' I said, interrupting in my turn, 'repeat my words. Say "I take this man, Francis Softly, for my lawful wedded husband." '

She repeated the sentence, with her face very pale, with her dear hand cold and trembling in mine.

'For better for worse,' continued the indomitable Mrs Baggs. 'Little enough of the better, I'm afraid, and Lord knows how much of the worse.'

I stopped her again with the promised five-pound note, and opened the room door. 'Now, ma'am,' I said, 'go to your room; take off your bonnet, and put your hair as tidy as you please.'

Mrs Baggs raised her eyes and hands to heaven, exclaimed 'Disgraceful!' and flounced out of the room in a passion. Such was my Scottish marriage – as lawful a ceremony, remember, as the finest family wedding at the largest parish church in all England.

An hour passed, and I had not yet summoned the cruel courage to communicate my real situation to Alicia. The entry of the shock-headed servant-girl to lay the cloth, followed by Mrs Baggs, who was never out of the way where eating and drinking appeared in prospect, helped me to rouse myself. I resolved to go out for a few minutes to reconnoitre, and make myself acquainted with any facilities for flight or hiding that the situation of the house might present. No doubt the Bow Street runner was lurking somewhere, but he must, as a matter of course, have heard, or informed himself, of the orders I had given relating to our conveyance on to Edinburgh; and, in that case, I was still no more in danger of his avowing himself and capturing me than I had been at any previous period of our journey.

'I am going out for a moment, love, to see about the chaise,' I said to Alicia. She suddenly looked up at me with an anxious searching expression. Was my face betraying anything of my real purpose? I hurried to the door before she could ask me a single question.

The front of the inn stood nearly in the middle of the principal street of the town. No chance of giving anyone the slip in that direction, and no sign, either, of the Bow Street runner. I sauntered round, with the most unconcerned manner I could assume, to the back of the house, by the inn yard. A door in one part of it stood half open. Inside was a bit of kitchen garden, bounded by a paling; beyond that some backs of detached houses; beyond them, again, a plot of weedy ground, a few wretched cottages, and the open, heathery moor. Good enough for running away, but terribly bad for hiding.

I returned disconsolately to the inn. Walking along the passage toward the staircase, I suddenly heard footsteps behind me – turned round, and saw the Bow Street runner (clothed again in his ordinary costume, and accompanied by two strange men) standing between me and the door.

'Sorry to stop you from going to Edinburgh, Mr Softly,' he said. 'But you're wanted back at Barkingham. I've just found out what you have been travelling all the way to Scotland for, and I take you prisoner, as one of the coining gang. Take it easy, sir. I've got help, you see, and you can't throttle three men, whatever you may have done at Barkingham with one.'

He handcuffed me as he spoke. Resistance was hopeless. I could only make an appeal to his mercy, on Alicia's account.

'Give me ten minutes,' I said, 'to break what has happened to my wife. We were only married an hour ago. If she knows this suddenly, it may be the death of her.'

'You've led me a nice dance on a wrong scent,' answered the runner, sulkily. 'But I never was a hard man where women are concerned. Go upstairs, and leave the door open, so that I can see in through it if I like. Hold your hat over your wrists, if you don't want her to see the handcuffs.'

I ascended the first flight of stairs, and my heart gave a sudden bound as if it would burst. I stopped, speechless and helpless, at the sight of Alicia, standing alone on the landing. My first look at her face told me she had heard all that had passed in the passage. She passionately struck the hat with which I had been trying to hide the handcuffs out of my fingers, and clasped me in her arms with such sudden and desperate energy that she absolutely hurt me.

'I was afraid of something, Frank,' she whispered. 'I followed you a little way. I stopped here; I have heard everything. Don't let us be parted! I am stronger than you think me. I won't be frightened. I won't cry. I won't trouble anybody, if that man will only take me with you!'

It is best for my sake, if not for the reader's, to hurry over the scene that followed.

It ended with as little additional wretchedness as could be expected. The runner was resolute about keeping me hand-cuffed and taking me back without a moment's unnecessary waste of time to Barkingham, but he relented on other points.

Where he was obliged to order a private conveyance, there was no objection to Alicia and Mrs Baggs following it. Where we got into a coach, there was no harm in their hiring two inside places. I gave my watch, rings, and last guinea to Alicia, enjoining her, on no account, to let her box of jewels see the light until we could get proper advice on the best means of turning them to account. She listened to these and other directions with a calmness that astonished me.

'You shan't say, my dear, that your wife has helped to make you uneasy by so much as a word or a look,' she whispered to me as we left the inn.

And she kept the hard promise implied in that one short sentence throughout the journey. Once only did I see her lose her self-possession. At starting on our way south, Mrs Baggs – taking the same incomprehensible personal offence at my misfortune that she had previously taken at the doctor's – upbraided me with my want of confidence in her, and declared that it was the main cause of all my present trouble. Alicia turned on her as she was uttering the words, with a look and a warning that silenced her in an instant: 'If you say another syllable that isn't kind to him, you shall find your way back by yourself!'

The words may not seem of much importance to others, but I thought, as I overheard them, that they justified every sacrifice I had made for my wife's sake.

XVI

On our way back I received from the runner some explanation of his apparently unaccountable proceedings in reference to myself.

To begin at the beginning, it turned out that the first act of the officers, on their release from the workroom in the red-brick house, was to institute a careful search for papers in the doctor's study and bedroom. Among the other documents that he had not had time to destroy was a letter to him from Alicia, which they took from one of the pockets of his dressing gown. Finding, from the report of the men who had followed the gig, that he had distanced all pursuit, and having therefore no direct clue to his whereabouts, they had been obliged to hunt after him in various directions, on pure speculation. Alicia's letter to her father gave the address of the house at Crickgelly, and to this the runner repaired, on the chance of intercepting or discovering any communications that the doctor might make to his daughter, Screw being taken with the officer to identify the young lady. After leaving the last coach, they posted to within a mile of Crickgelly, and then walked into the village, in order to excite no special attention, should the doctor be lurking in the neighbourhood. The runner had tried ineffectually to gain admission as a visitor at Zion Place. After having the door shut on him, he and Screw had watched the house and village, and had seen me approach number two. Their suspicions were directly excited.

Thus far, Screw had not recognised, nor even observed me; but he immediately identified me by my voice, while I was parleying with the stupid servant at the door. The runner, hearing who I was, reasonably enough concluded that I must be the recognised medium of communication between the doctor and his daughter, especially when he found that I was admitted instantly after calling, past the servant, to someone inside the house.

Leaving Screw on the watch, he went to the inn, discovered himself privately to the landlord, and made sure (in more ways than one, as I conjectured) of knowing when, and in what direction, I should leave Crickgelly. On finding that I was to leave it the next morning, with Alicia and Mrs Baggs, he immediately suspected that I was charged with the duty of taking the daughter to, or near, the place chosen for the father's retreat, and had therefore abstained from interfering prematurely with my movements. Knowing whither we were bound in the cart, he had ridden after us, well out of sight, with his countryman's disguise ready for use in the saddle-bags – Screw, in case of any mistakes or mystifications, being left behind on the watch at Crickgelly.

The possibility that I might be running away with Alicia had suggested itself to him, but he dismissed it as improbable, first when he saw that Mrs Baggs accompanied us, and again, when, on nearing Scotland, he found that we did not take the road to Gretna Green. He acknowledged, in conclusion, that he should have followed us to Edinburgh, or even to the Continent itself, on the chance of our leading him to the doctor's retreat, but for the servant-girl at the inn, who had listened outside the door while our brief marriage ceremony was proceeding, and from whom, with great trouble and delay, he had extracted all the information he required. A further loss of half an hour's time had occurred while he was getting the necessary help to assist him, in the event of my resisting, or trying to give him the slip, in making me a prisoner. These small facts accounted for the hour's respite we had enjoyed at the inn, and terminated the runner's narrative of his own proceedings.

On arriving at our destination I was, of course, immediately taken to the jail.

Alicia, by my advice, engaged a modest lodging in a suburb of Barkingham. In the days of the red-brick house, she had seldom been seen in the town, and she was not at all known by sight in the suburb. We arranged that she was to visit me as often as the authorities would let her. She had no companion, and wanted none. Mrs Baggs, who had never forgiven the rebuke administered to her at the starting-point of our journey, left us at the close of it. Her leave-taking was dignified and pathetic. She kindly informed Alicia that she wished her well, though she could not conscientiously look upon her as a lawful married woman, and she begged me (in case I got off), the next time I met with a respectable person who was kind to me, to profit by remembering my past errors, and to treat my next benefactress with more confidence than I had treated her.

My first business in the prison was to write to Mr Batterbury.

I had a magnificent ease to present to him, this time. Although I believed myself, and had succeeded in persuading Alicia, that I was sure of being recommended to mercy, it was not the less the fact that I was charged with an offence still punishable by death, in the then barbarous state of the law. I delicately stated just enough of my case to make one thing clear to the mind of Mr Batterbury. My affectionate sister's interest in the contingent reversion was now (unless Lady Malkinshaw perversely and suddenly expired) actually threatened by the gallows!

While calmly awaiting the answer, I was by no means without subjects to occupy my attention when Alicia was not at the prison. There was my fellow-workman – Mill – (the first member of our society betrayed by Screw) to compare notes with, and there was a certain prisoner who had been transported, and who had some very important and interesting particulars to communicate, relative to life and its chances in our felon-settlements at the Antipodes. I talked a great deal with this man, for I felt that his experience might be of the greatest possible benefit to me.

Mr Batterbury's answer was speedy, short, and punctual. I had shattered his nervous system forever, he wrote, but had only stimulated his devotion to my family, and his Christian readiness to look pityingly on my transgressions. He had engaged the leader of the circuit to defend me, and he would have come to see me, but for Mrs Batterbury, who had implored him not to expose himself to agitation. Of Lady Malkinshaw the letter said nothing, but I afterward discovered that she was then at Cheltenham, drinking the waters and playing whist in the rudest health and spirits.

It is a bold thing to say, but nothing will ever persuade me that society has not a sneaking kindness for a Rogue.

For example, my father never had half the attention shown to him in his own house, which was shown to me in my prison. I have seen high sheriffs in the great world, whom my father went to see, give him two fingers – the High Sheriff of Barkinghamshire came to see me, and shook hands cordially. Nobody ever wanted my father's autograph – dozens of people asked for mine. Nobody ever put my father's portrait in the frontispiece of a magazine, or described his personal appearance and manners with anxious elaboration, in the large type of a great newspaper – I enjoyed both those honours. Three official individuals politely begged me to be sure and make complaints if my position was not perfectly comfortable. No official individual ever troubled his head whether my father was comfortable or not. When the day of my trial came, the court was thronged by my lovely countrywomen, who stood up panting in the crowd and crushing their beautiful dresses, rather than miss the pleasure of seeing the dear Rogue in the dock. When my father once stood on the lecturer's rostrum and delivered his excellent discourse, called 'Medical Hints to Maids and Mothers on Tight Lacing and Teething,' the benches were left empty by the ungrateful women of England, who were not in the slightest degree anxious to feast their eyes on the sight of a learned adviser and respectable man. If these facts led to one inevitable conclusion, it is not my fault. We Rogues are the spoiled children of society. We may not be openly acknowledged as pets, but we all know, by pleasant experience, that we are treated like them.

The trial was deeply affecting. My defence – or rather my barrister's – was the simple truth. It was impossible to overthrow the facts against us, so we honestly owned that I got into the scrape through love for Alicia. My counsel turned this to the best possible sentimental account. He cried; the ladies cried; the jury cried; the judge cried; and Mr Batterbury, who had desperately come to see the trial, and know the worst, sobbed with such prominent vehemence that I believe him, to this day, to have greatly influenced the verdict. I was strongly recommended to mercy and got off with fourteen years' transportation. The unfortunate Mill, who was tried after me, with a mere dry-eyed barrister to defend him, was hanged.

POSTSCRIPT

With the record of my sentence of transportation, my life as a Rogue ends, and my existence as a respectable man begins. I am sorry to say anything that may disturb popular delusions on the subject of poetical justice, but this is strictly the truth.

My first anxiety was about my wife's future.

Mr Batterbury gave me no chance of asking his advice after the trial. The moment sentence had been pronounced, he allowed himself to be helped out of court in a melancholy state of prostration, and the next morning he left for London. I suspect he was afraid to face me, and nervously impatient, besides, to tell Annabella that he had saved the legacy again by another alarming sacrifice. My father and mother, to whom I had written on the subject of Alicia, were no more to be depended on than Mr Batterbury. My father, in answering my letter, told me that he conscientiously believed he had done enough in forgiving me for throwing away an excellent education, and disgracing a respectable name. He added that he had not allowed my letter for my mother to reach her, out of pitying regard for her broken health and spirits, and he ended by telling me (what was perhaps very true) that the wife of such a son as I had been had no claim upon her father-in-law's protection and help. There was an end, then, of any hope of finding resources for Alicia among the members of my own family.

The next thing was to discover a means of providing for her without assistance. I had formed a project for this, after meditating over my conversations with the returned transport in Barkingham jail, and I had taken a reliable opinion on the chances of successfully executing my design from the solicitor who had prepared my defence.

Alicia herself was so earnestly in favour of assisting in my experiment that she declared she would prefer death to its abandonment. Accordingly, the necessary preliminaries were arranged, and, when we parted, it was some mitigation of our grief to know that there was a time appointed for meeting again. Alicia was to lodge with a distant relative of her mother's in a suburb of London, was to concert measures with this relative on the best method of turning her jewels into money, and was to follow her convict husband to the Antipodes, under a feigned name, in six months' time.

If my family had not abandoned me, I need not have thus left her to help herself. As it was, I had no choice. One consolation supported me at parting – she was in no danger of persecution from her father. A second letter from him had arrived at Crickgelly, and had been forwarded to the address I had left for it. It was dated Hamburg, and briefly told her to remain at Crickgelly, and expect fresh instructions, explanations, and a supply of money, as soon as he had settled the important business matters that had taken him abroad. His daughter answered the letter, telling him of her marriage, and giving him an address at a post office to write to, if he chose to reply to her communication. There the matter rested.

What was I to do on my side? Nothing but establish a reputation for mild behaviour. I began to manufacture a character for myself for the first days of our voyage out in the convict-ship, and I landed at the penal settlement with the reputation of being the meekest and most biddable of felonious mankind.

After a short probationary experience of such low convict employments as lime-burning and road-mending, I was advanced to occupations more in harmony with my education. Whatever I did, I never neglected the first great obligation of making myself agreeable and amusing to everybody. My social reputation as a good fellow began to stand as high at one end of the world as ever it stood at the other. The months passed more quickly than I had dared to hope. The expiration of my first year of transportation was approaching, and already pleasant hints of my being soon assigned to private service began to reach my ears. This was the first of the many ends I was now working for, and the next pleasant realisation of my hopes that I had to expect was the arrival of Alicia.

She came, a month later than I had anticipated, safe and blooming, with five hundred pounds as the produce of her jewels, and with the old Crickgelly alias (changed from Miss to Mrs Giles), to prevent any suspicions of the connection between us.

Her story (concocted by me before I left England) was that she was a widow lady who had come to settle in Australia, and make the most of her little property in the New World. One of the first things Mrs Giles wanted was necessarily a trustworthy servant, and she had to make her choice of one among the convicts of good character, to be assigned to private service. Being one of that honourable body myself at the time, it is needless to say that I was the fortunate man on whom Mrs Giles's choice fell. The first situation I got in Australia was as servant to my own wife.

Alicia made a very indulgent mistress.

If she had been mischievously inclined, she might, by application to a magistrate, have had me flogged or set to work in chains on the roads, whenever I became idle or insubordinate, which happened occasionally. But instead of complaining, the kind creature kissed and made much of her footman by stealth, after his day's work. She allowed him no female followers, and only employed one woman-servant occasionally, who was both old and ugly. The name of the footman was Dear in private, and Francis in company, and when the widowed mistress, upstairs, refused eligible offers of marriage (which was pretty often), the favoured domestic in the kitchen was always informed of it and asked, with the sweetest humility, if he approved of the proceeding.

Not to dwell on this anomalous period of my existence, let me say briefly that my new position with my wife was of the greatest advantage in enabling me to direct in secret the profitable uses to which her little fortune was put.

We began in this way with an excellent speculation in cattle – buying them for shillings and selling them for pounds. With the profits thus obtained, we next tried our hands at houses – first buying in a small way, then boldly building, and letting again and selling to great advantage. While these speculations were in progress, my behaviour in my wife's service was so exemplary, and she gave me so excellent a character when the usual official enquiries were instituted, that I soon got the next privilege accorded to persons in my situation – a ticket of leave. By the time this had been again exchanged for a conditional pardon (which allowed me to go about where I pleased in Australia, and to trade in my own name like any unconvicted merchant) our house-property had increased enormously, our land had been sold for public buildings, and we had shares in the famous Emancipist's Bank, which produced quite a little income of themselves.

There was now no need to keep the mask on any longer.

I went through the superfluous ceremony of a second marriage with Alicia; took stores in the city; built a villa in the country; and here I am at this present moment of writing, a convict aristocrat – a prosperous, wealthy, highly respectable mercantile man, with two years of my sentence of transportation still to expire. I have a barouche and two bay horses, a coachman and page in neat liveries, three charming children, and a French governess, a boudoir and lady's maid for my wife. She is as handsome as ever, but getting a little fat. So am I, as a worthy friend remarked when I recently appeared holding the plate, at our last charity sermon.

What would my surviving relatives and associates in England say, if they could see me now? I have heard of them at different times and through various channels. Lady Malkinshaw, after living to the verge of a hundred and surviving all sorts of accidents, died quietly one afternoon, in her chair, with an empty dish before her, and without giving the slightest notice to anybody. Mr Batterbury, having sacrificed so much to his wife's reversion, profited nothing by its falling in at last. His quarrels with my amiable sister – which took their rise from his interested charities toward me – ended in producing a separation. And, far from saving anything by Annabella's inheritance of her pin money, he had a positive loss to put up with, in the shape of some hundreds extracted yearly from his income, as alimony to his uncongenial wife. He is said to make use of shocking language whenever my name is mentioned, and to wish that he had been carried off by the yellow fever before he ever set eyes on the Softly family.

My father has retired from practice. He and my mother have gone to live in the country, near the mansion of the only marquis with whom my father was actually and personally acquainted in his professional days. The marquis asks him to dinner once a year, and leaves a card for my mother before he returns to town for the season. A portrait of Lady Malkinshaw hangs in the dining room. In this way, my parents are ending their days contentedly. I can honestly say that I am glad to hear it.

Dr Dulcifer, when I last heard of him, was editing a newspaper in America. Old File, who shared his flight, still shares his fortunes, being publisher of his newspaper. Young File resumed coining operations in London, and, having braved his fate a second time, threaded his way, in due course, up to the steps of the scaffold. Screw carries on the profitable trade of informer, in London. The dismal disappearance of Mill I have already recorded.

So much on the subject of my relatives and associates. On the subject of myself, I might still write on at considerable length. But while the libellous title of 'A Rogue's Life' stares me in the face at the top of the page, how can I, as a rich and reputable man, be expected to communicate any further autobiographical particulars, in this place, to a discerning public of readers? No, no, my friends! I am no longer interesting – I am only respectable like yourselves. It is time to say 'goodbye'.

NOTES

1. Charles Dickens established the weekly magazine *Household Words* with his London publishers Bradbury and Evans. It ran from 1850 to 1859.

2. Writer Charles Reade (1814–84).

3. A member of the Comédie Française and the Théâtre Français, playwright Regnier collaborated with Collins on a dramatisation of his 1866 novel *Armadale*.

4. French landscape painter Claude Lorrain (1600–82).

5. Dutch painter Rembrandt (1606–69); Italian painter Raphael (1483–1520); Venetian painter Titian (*c.*1490–1576); Dutch painter Albert Cuyp (1620–91); French painter Antoine Watteau (1684–1721).

6. Belgian painters David Teniers the Elder (1582–1649) and the Younger (1610–90).

7. The death of John the Baptist is reported in the synoptic gospels. Salome, the daughter of Herod's wife Herodias, so pleased Herod with her dancing that he promised her anything she wished. Herodias prompted her daughter to ask for the death of John the Baptist. Herod granted her wish and John was beheaded.

8. *The Adventures of Gil Blas of Santillane* by French writer Alain René Lesage (1668–1747). A picaresque novel, it was translated into English by Tobias Smollett, and was both popular and widely influential.

BIOGRAPHICAL NOTE

William Wilkie Collins, author of the first detective novels in English, was born in 1824. The son of a respected landscape painter, he was named after his painter godfather, David Wilkie. Educated in London, Collins studied to become a barrister, although it was never his intention to practise, and by 1848 he had turned to writing, a number of short works appearing in Charles Dickens' periodicals, *Household Words* and, later, *All the Year Round*. A first novel, *Iolani*, set in ancient Tahiti and involving sorcery and sacrifice, though perhaps written as early as 1844, was later rejected by publishers (and only rediscovered and published for the first time in 1999). His second novel, *Antonina* (1850), set in fifth-century Rome, was a popular success, before Collins' first venture into crime fiction with *Basil* (1852), a Gothic tale of doppelgangers, bigamy, and hidden family secrets. Developing at once detective fiction and the novel of sensation, Collins' exotic and gripping stories – often involving strong heroines, sinister locales, charlatans, and physical or psychological afflictions – became hugely popular with the reading public. His great novels appeared in the 1860s, when, at the height of his powers, Collins' wrote *The Woman in White* (1860), *No Name* (1862), *Armadale* (1866), and *The Moonstone* (1868).

Unafraid to question Victorian social mores, Collins never married but maintained two families. He lived both with Caroline Graves (whom he met in a midnight encounter such as is described in *The Woman in White*) and with Martha Rudd. In later life, Collins became addicted to opium, and the novels he wrote between 1870 and 1889 – concerned with social issues – are considered inferior to his earlier output.

SELECTED TITLES FROM HESPERUS PRESS

Author	Title	Foreword writer
Pietro Aretino	*The School of Whoredom*	Paul Bailey
Pietro Aretino	*The Secret Life of Nuns*	
Jane Austen	*Lesley Castle*	Zoë Heller
Jane Austen	*Love and Friendship*	Fay Weldon
Honoré de Balzac	*Colonel Chabert*	A.N. Wilson
Charles Baudelaire	*On Wine and Hashish*	Margaret Drabble
Giovanni Boccaccio	*Life of Dante*	A.N. Wilson
Charlotte Brontë	*The Spell*	
Emily Brontë	*Poems of Solitude*	Helen Dunmore
Mikhail Bulgakov	*Fatal Eggs*	Doris Lessing
Mikhail Bulgakov	*The Heart of a Dog*	A.S. Byatt
Giacomo Casanova	*The Duel*	Tim Parks
Miguel de Cervantes	*The Dialogue of the Dogs*	Ben Okri
Geoffrey Chaucer	*The Parliament of Birds*	
Anton Chekhov	*The Story of a Nobody*	Louis de Bernières
Anton Chekhov	*Three Years*	William Fiennes
Wilkie Collins	*The Frozen Deep*	
Joseph Conrad	*Heart of Darkness*	A.N. Wilson
Joseph Conrad	*The Return*	Colm Tóibín
Gabriele D'Annunzio	*The Book of the Virgins*	Tim Parks
Dante Alighieri	*The Divine Comedy: Inferno*	
Dante Alighieri	*New Life*	Louis de Bernières
Daniel Defoe	*The King of Pirates*	Peter Ackroyd
Marquis de Sade	*Incest*	Janet Street-Porter
Charles Dickens	*The Haunted House*	Peter Ackroyd
Charles Dickens	*A House to Let*	
Fyodor Dostoevsky	*The Double*	Jeremy Dyson
Fyodor Dostoevsky	*Poor People*	Charlotte Hobson
Alexandre Dumas	*One Thousand and One Ghosts*	

George Eliot	*Amos Barton*	Matthew Sweet
Henry Fielding	*Jonathan Wild the Great*	Peter Ackroyd
F. Scott Fitzgerald	*The Popular Girl*	Helen Dunmore
Gustave Flaubert	*Memoirs of a Madman*	Germaine Greer
Ugo Foscolo	*Last Letters of Jacopo Ortis*	Valerio Massimo Manfredi
Elizabeth Gaskell	*Lois the Witch*	Jenny Uglow
Théophile Gautier	*The Jinx*	Gilbert Adair
André Gide	*Theseus*	
Johann Wolfgang von Goethe	*The Man of Fifty*	A.S. Byatt
Nikolai Gogol	*The Squabble*	Patrick McCabe
E.T.A. Hoffmann	*Mademoiselle de Scudéri*	Gilbert Adair
Victor Hugo	*The Last Day of a Condemned Man*	Libby Purves
Joris-Karl Huysmans	*With the Flow*	Simon Callow
Henry James	*In the Cage*	Libby Purves
Franz Kafka	*Metamorphosis*	Martin Jarvis
Franz Kafka	*The Trial*	Zadie Smith
John Keats	*Fugitive Poems*	Andrew Motion
Heinrich von Kleist	*The Marquise of O–*	Andrew Miller
Mikhail Lermontov	*A Hero of Our Time*	Doris Lessing
Nikolai Leskov	*Lady Macbeth of Mtsensk*	Gilbert Adair
Carlo Levi	*Words are Stones*	Anita Desai
Xavier de Maistre	*A Journey Around my Room*	Alain de Botton
André Malraux	*The Way of the Kings*	Rachel Seiffert
Katherine Mansfield	*Prelude*	William Boyd
Edgar Lee Masters	*Spoon River Anthology*	Shena Mackay
Guy de Maupassant	*Butterball*	Germaine Greer
Prosper Mérimée	*Carmen*	Philip Pullman
Sir Thomas More	*The History of King Richard III*	Sister Wendy Beckett

Sándor Petőfi	*John the Valiant*	George Szirtes
Francis Petrarch	*My Secret Book*	Germaine Greer
Luigi Pirandello	*Loveless Love*	
Edgar Allan Poe	*Eureka*	Sir Patrick Moore
Alexander Pope	*The Rape of the Lock and A Key to the Lock*	Peter Ackroyd
Antoine-François Prévost	*Manon Lescaut*	Germaine Greer
Marcel Proust	*Pleasures and Days*	A.N. Wilson
Alexander Pushkin	*Dubrovsky*	Patrick Neate
Alexander Pushkin	*Ruslan and Lyudmila*	Colm Tóibín
François Rabelais	*Pantagruel*	Paul Bailey
François Rabelais	*Gargantua*	Paul Bailey
Christina Rossetti	*Commonplace*	Andrew Motion
George Sand	*The Devil's Pool*	Victoria Glendinning
Jean-Paul Sartre	*The Wall*	Justin Cartwright
Friedrich von Schiller	*The Ghost-seer*	Martin Jarvis
Mary Shelley	*Transformation*	
Percy Bysshe Shelley	*Zastrozzi*	Germaine Greer
Stendhal	*Memoirs of an Egotist*	Doris Lessing
Robert Louis Stevenson	*Dr Jekyll and Mr Hyde*	Helen Dunmore
Theodor Storm	*The Lake of the Bees*	Alan Sillitoe
Leo Tolstoy	*The Death of Ivan Ilych*	
Leo Tolstoy	*Hadji Murat*	Colm Tóibín
Ivan Turgenev	*Faust*	Simon Callow
Mark Twain	*The Diary of Adam and Eve*	John Updike
Mark Twain	*Tom Sawyer, Detective*	
Oscar Wilde	*The Portrait of Mr W.H.*	Peter Ackroyd
Virginia Woolf	*Carlyle's House and Other Sketches*	Doris Lessing
Virginia Woolf	*Monday or Tuesday*	Scarlett Thomas
Emile Zola	*For a Night of Love*	A.N. Wilson